THE DEADLY CIRCLE

A PARKER LEE MYSTERY

M.P. BLACK

Dear reader, I dedicate this book to you.

Thank you.

1

It began with a whisper: "Hey, Park."

Someone tapped me on the shoulder. My brother Scottie, sitting in the pew behind me. I frowned at him and raised a finger to my lips. Typical of Scottie to be talking during the Sunday service.

I turned back around, focusing my attention on my sister Amy.

Amy, pastor at Shepherd's Gate Church, was standing by the lectern. She wore a white robe with a stole hanging over her shoulders. Light from the tall stained-glass windows behind her shone down on her.

"I want to tell you a story," she told us, her congregation, her amplified voice reverberating into the rafters. "It comes to us from the stories of Buddha. It's about Aṅgulimāla, a cruel brigand. A killer."

She told the story of the brigand, and how he took the first steps toward redemption by becoming a monk—and then, helping a woman through a difficult childbirth, he became a man who brought life instead of death to the village.

Before Amy even finished the lesson, I got her point: even the worst of us could find redemption through our actions. A classic Amy sermon. And I was thinking about how it might apply to my own life, when Scottie tapped my shoulder again.

I turned around. "Settle down," I hissed.

"But, Park—"

He motioned at something beyond me. What was he pointing at? Despite my irritation, I turned to look. My curiosity usually trumps my annoyance—even at Scottie, who can be pretty annoying.

He was gesturing at someone, not something. A man sitting a few pews ahead of us, across the aisle. Short, black hair. Oxford shirt, untucked. Jeans. Loafers. No socks. Even seeing only his profile, I recognized him.

I sucked in my breath.

"It's him," Scottie said, "isn't it?"

I nodded. "Ken Tora."

Ken Tora wasn't just famous in Allington. People all over the country—all over the world—knew about Ken Tora. He was one of those Silicon Valley start-up dudes whose name had become synonymous with easy money and fast-lane success. In Allington, of course, he was proudly remembered as "one of ours." Born and raised.

"What's he doing back in Allington?" I wondered out loud.

"I don't know. But we should find out. And I'm definitely pitching at least one business idea to him."

I winced. Scottie wasn't kidding. On top of owning Scottie's Ice Cream Shop and Allington Bike Rentals, my youngest of two older brothers always had half a dozen side hustles and a hundred startup ideas floating around.

"Before you scare him off, let me talk to him first," I said. "Can you imagine if I landed an interview with Ken Tora?"

"Dad would be happy."

"So would *The Gazette*'s readers," I said.

"Shh..." Mom, who sat to my left, nudged me.

To her left sat Joy, my other sister. Next to her was Ray, my oldest brother. Dad was the last one in the pew.

If you lived in Allington, you couldn't escape the Lee family. Mom was the chief of police of our little town. Joy ran Café Larke and Pure Joy Yoga Studio on Peony Lane. Ray owned the Lake Breeze Brewery—or simply "The Breeze" to us locals—right down on the docks near Scottie's Ice Cream Shop. And Dad owned *The Allington Gazette*, where I worked as the only full-time reporter.

As a teen, I'd felt stifled by my family. They were, quite literally, everywhere I turned. So I'd escaped to college and after that to the big city to work at a national newspaper.

But I lost my job and came home, with my tail tucked between my legs.

Only to discover that Allington was pretty neat.

Maybe Ken Tora was discovering the same thing. In fact, he looked engrossed in Amy's story about the brigand-turned-monk. Mesmerized. The only times he took his eyes off my sister, he bent over a notebook and scribbled furiously.

When the service ended and the coffee hour began, Ken shot to his feet and pushed through the crowd toward my sister. On my side of the aisle, it took longer to get out.

I wove my way past the congregants, and by the time I got to Amy and Ken, they were deep in conversation already. I waited. No point interrupting. In fact, I wanted to make a good impression.

Amy said, "I'm happy to meet with you, if you'd like to talk more."

Ken scratched his neck. "I guess that'd be good…"

"Come to my office after coffee hour."

She smiled at him. His own smile was weak. Uncertain. Not the kind of smile I was used to seeing in news articles or on social. Where was the confident Ken Tora I knew from the media?

He turned away from Amy. Here was my chance. Out of the corner of my eye, I spotted a familiar figure swooping in. Scottie. As quickly as I could, I grabbed Ken's arm and spun him away from Scottie.

"Ken," I said, as if we were old friends. "Could we talk? I'm from *The Allington Gazette*, and I'd love to—"

He stiffened, his eyes widening.

"No," he muttered, pulling his arm from my grasp. "Not right now."

Inwardly, I cursed myself. Too direct. Barreling right into the topic.

He ducked past me. Scottie bore down on him. But Ken must have an elevator-pitch radar, because he swerved around my brother, and like a halfback speeding down the football field, streaked down the aisle. Heading straight for the exit.

Ken stopped. A sudden, jarring stop. A man with slicked-back hair and an angular, fox-like face leaned against the doorway, his arms crossed. Smiling at Ken.

As Ken approached—slowly, cautiously—the guy nodded at him and threw an arm around his shoulders. Even at a distance, I could see he gripped Ken firmly, guiding him out of the church.

Before vanishing into the bright Sunday sunshine, Ken

cast a glance backward, a frown on his face. A worried frown. I stared at the emptiness he left behind, wondering what could worry Ken Tora.

"Bummer," Scottie said. "Next time, eh, Park?"

"Yeah. Next time."

2

From one of the Lakeview Inn's rooms on the second floor, Aunt Lil and I had a perfect view of Lake Allington. The restored Victorian mansion stood at the edge of the lake between the town and the woods.

High above us, a single-propeller airplane belonging to our local tour company droned across the sky. White-sailed boats cut through the rippling waters. Birds bobbed on the surface near Gull Island. And wafting on the breeze: the smell of pine trees in sunshine.

But my attention was on the back porch below us. Ken Tora was sitting at a table near the railing, hunched over his leather-bound notebook.

I had a good reason to be in this room on the second floor. First, Aunt Lil was the owner of the inn. And second, she was my aunt. I'd suggested I could help her make the room ready for incoming guests this afternoon. Which, of course, Zadie, the housekeeper, had already done. And since she'd done everything that needed doing, why not look out the window and enjoy the view out the window?

"He's reading," I whispered, leaning over the windowsill to get a better view. "No, hold on. He picked up his pen. Now he's writing."

"Amazing," Aunt Lil said. "These celebrities are almost human."

"Ha, ha. But seriously, Lil, this is a big deal. This is Ken Tora."

Aunt Lil wore a billowy muumuu with a pentagram pattern all over. Half a dozen necklaces with various pendants hung around her neck. She waved a hand dismissively at my comment, jangling her many bangles.

"I know all about Ken Tora," she said.

"You do?"

"Can't you see? The Saturn-Pluto conjunction looms over him. Saturn tests his resilience, while Pluto heralds transformation, whispering of secrets and hidden struggles."

I pulled back from the window and put a hand on my hip, giving Aunt Lil my best frown. "If you've had time to do his astrological reading, you must've known about him for a while. Why didn't you tell me *the* Ken Tora was coming to stay at the inn?"

"I didn't know you were such a fan."

"Not a fan? He was on TIME Magazine's 30 Under 30 list. He's one of Allington's most famous exports. Imagine if I could get an interview with him." I sighed. "But that's a big *if*."

I told her about my attempt to talk to him at church earlier that morning.

As I talked she gazed at me, squinting a little. Was she even listening to me?

She dug into her bag, rooted around, and pulled out a

crystal stick. It was her selenite—or moonstone—wand. She waved it all around me.

"If you don't take care of your aura, Parker, who will?" She sighed. When she was finished cleaning my aura, she put her wand back in her bag. "Anyway, why worry about Ken Tora? If you don't catch him this time, you'll get him next year."

"Next year?"

"He and his friends come back to Allington once a year for a reunion."

My jaw dropped. "For how long?"

"A week."

Aunt Lil kept tabs on town gossip. But she didn't always share the stuff I found newsworthy. She often seemed more interested in planetary alignments.

This was helpful information. A week was plenty of time. I made a promise to myself: before that week was over, I would get a story out of Ken Tora.

"Come on," I said, heading for the door.

"Where are we going now?"

"Downstairs. I want to get closer to Ken. Maybe I'll get another chance to talk to him."

We left the room and headed down the corridor. As we came down the stairs to the reception, we bumped into a man in green overalls with a cap on his head. The inn's gardener. He was a jowly, unshaven man in his late 50s, with a pair of thick, wide lips that made him look like a toad. His unibrow was just as thick.

He was carrying a fishing rod and a tackle box.

"Mr. Groff," Aunt Lil said, eyeing the fishing rod. "Aren't you supposed to be digging up those flowerbeds today?"

Mr. Groff snorted. "I would if I could. But someone's been in the toolshed. My shovel's gone."

"You mean *my* shovel, Mr. Groff? And how do you know it was stolen? Your nature as a Scorpio makes you suspicious and quick to blame others. Anyway—" Aunt Lil made a dismissive gesture with her hand, bangles rattling. "—it's probably lying around somewhere. I'll get another. Meanwhile, you're the gardener—don't you have a shovel of your own?"

He glared at her, clearly insulted by her astrological analysis. "Not with me. You expect me to lug that stuff around to every client?"

I was tempted to say, "Uh, yeah." But I held my tongue. This was Aunt Lil's business. She could handle it.

"So typical of a Scorpio to say that," she said with a smile. "So, what are you working on today?"

Mr. Groff shrugged. "Nothing. Until that shovel turns up, I'm going to do some fishing." He raised the rod and tackle box, in case we hadn't noticed them yet. "Now, if you're done interrogating me..."

He lumbered past us. I stared at his back as he wandered down the corridor toward the dining room, where he disappeared through a door. A creak followed by a slap-bang told me he'd gone out the back to the porch. From there, he could walk straight down a set of stairs to the inn's dock.

"Unbelievable," I said. "His behavior—just unbelievable."

"Not if you've worked with Gordon Groff before," Aunt Lil said. "I ought to fire him. But when he works, he does a good job, and he's affordable. And Scorpios can be very loyal." Then she frowned. "Come to think of it, they can be wonderfully perceptive, even intuitive."

"And cheerful, too?"

Aunt Lil laughed. "That's one thing Mr. Groff's never been accused of."

A memory tickled the back of my mind. Something about a Mr. Gordon Groff being accused of something. I frowned. Then shook my head. Probably some other Groff.

3

Aunt Lil stayed in the reception to welcome a newly arrived guest. Out on the Lakeview Inn's back porch, I casually positioned myself at the railing. As if I were enjoying the view.

Out on the lake, sail boats drifting lazily past. A canoe gliding into view from behind Gull Island, the little lump of rocks and trees about a mile out. My attention was only half on the view. I stood close enough to Ken that I could look over his shoulder.

If he noticed me, Ken didn't let on. He was still engrossed in his notebook. Scribbling. Then flipping back a few pages to read. Then returning to a blank page and writing again.

Below me, Gordon Groff sat on the edge of the dock, his thick legs dangling over the water. He held his fishing rod. The line reached far into the lake where he'd cast it. He glared at it, as if it had offended him. But after a while, he glanced up. A quick glance. Then back down to his fishing line.

Was he keeping an eye on me?

Again, I wondered what story I'd once heard about him. Once I was back at my desk at *The Gazette,* I could look him up.

While I watched Groff, I also noticed a rowboat coming toward the dock. Two women—I'd say both somewhere in their mid-20s—one pulling on the oars, the other leaning back and trailing a hand in the water.

The boat bumped against the dock. The one who'd been lounging grabbed the rope, jumped onto the dock, and tied up the boat. She yanked at the rope, securing it firmly. Confidently.

She wore practical clothes: sneakers, a pair of hiking pants, and a tight-fitting tank-top with a loose shirt over it. A purple baseball cap over her long black hair.

The other woman—a big head of unruly bird's nest hair, and a colorful cotton scarf tossed around her neck—held her arms out to maintain her balance. She took one step, then another. The boat rocked and she let out a strangled cry.

"I'm going to fall in," she said, her voice high-pitched with worry.

"Take it easy, Judy," the other woman said. She stuck out a hand. "You're doing great."

Judy grabbed her friend's hand, a row of bangles on her wrists jingling and jangling. They reminded me of Aunt Lil's. Judy allowed herself to be hauled up to the dock.

"Thanks, Priscilla. I just don't like boats. I just—"

Gordon Groff, sitting on the opposite side of the dock, turned around to scowl at the women. Maybe they were scaring away his fish.

But then something happened. Groff's eyes widened. The woman named Judy let out a moan and put a hand to her mouth.

"It's him," she said.

Her friend Priscilla glanced over at Groff. Frowned. Apparently recognizing him, too. Then grabbed Judy by the arm and hauled her away, hurrying down the dock.

Groff struggled to his feet, huffing. Still holding his fishing rod.

"Hold on," he said. "Listen to me…"

"Come on," Priscilla said, guiding Judy up the stairs that connected the back porch to the dock.

Judy cast an anxious glance over her shoulder at Groff.

Priscilla tugged at her. "Ignore him. He can't follow you. Or we'll call the cops."

"No." Judy's voice was barely audible. "No…"

"It won't come to that. But he knows. So he'll stay where he is."

Priscilla hauled Judy onto the back porch. Apparently she knew what she was talking about, because Groff stayed on the dock, staring up at them. A strange mixture of anger and confusion on his face. His wide lips working. Like he was chewing on something.

Priscilla, still gripping Judy's arm, headed for Ken's table.

"Go ahead and sit down, Judy," she said. "I'll see about drinks."

Priscilla slipped inside the inn, and a minute later, she re-emerged with Aunt Lil behind her. Aunt Lil said, "I'm sorry if Mr. Groff was bothering you somehow. I'm happy to speak to him."

"That won't be necessary," Priscilla said. She motioned toward Judy and rolled her eyes. Gestures intended only for Lil. "Judy just needs to calm down."

Aunt Lil nodded, apparently understanding. I did too: Judy must be high-strung. She seemed anxious. She was sitting down next to Ken now, fidgeting with the bangles on her wrists.

Aunt Lil said, "In any case, I can get those drinks for you. What would you like?"

Priscilla smiled. "Thanks so much. We appreciate it. We feel well taken care of here."

"That's the whole point."

Without consulting the others, Priscilla gave Aunt Lil their order—coffee for Priscilla and Ken, plus an herbal tea for Judy—and she went inside.

I stayed at the railing. Still pretending to admire the view.

Priscilla sat down next to Judy, across from Ken. She gave Judy a little nudge.

"You'll be fine," she said.

"It was such a shock..."

"...but nothing a chamomile tea can't cure," Priscilla said, finishing Judy's sentence. But also mimicking her voice. The imitation was incredible. Eerily like Judy.

"Cut it out," Ken said. But Priscilla ignored him.

The imitation made Judy smile. A weak smile, but still a smile.

"Stop it, Priscilla," she said.

"That's better," Priscilla said. "If your chamomile won't cure the shock, your smile will."

The lounge door opened. I expected Lil. Instead two men—also in their 20s—emerged. One of them was the fox-faced man with slicked back hair who'd met Ken at the church. The other, hurrying after his friend, sported a messy bedhead. Intentional or not. And his droopy basset-hound eyes scanned the people at the table on the porch.

"Hey, guys," he said, a smile spreading across his face.

Ken, Priscilla, and Judy occupied three of the four chairs

at the table. The fox-faced guy grabbed the fourth, the one next to Ken.

He said, "Trevor, go find a chair for yourself."

"You bet, Jack," Trevor, with the messy hair, said. Bobbing his head, and like a well-trained puppy, he hurried off to get a chair from another table. He dragged it back over and sat down at the end of the table.

"So," he said, looking eagerly at each of them. "What's going on?"

These must be Ken's friends—the reunion Lil mentioned: Judy, Priscilla, Jack, and Trevor. Priscilla and Judy faced me. Trevor was in profile. Ken and Jack had their backs to me.

Jack said, "Ken, why don't you tell everyone what you were doing at church this morning?"

Ken shrugged. "Can't I go to church if I want?"

"And talk to the pastor."

"We were chatting. That's all."

"About what? Aṅgulimāla, the cruel brigand?" Jack snorted. "I didn't know you were into that spiritual crap."

Ken pushed back his chair. "I don't need this."

Jack put a hand on his arm. "Hey, buddy. Calm down. I was just joking."

Just then, Aunt Lil emerged from inside with a tray. She distributed the drinks. Two coffees and a cup of tea. And then took orders from Jack and Trevor.

While Aunt Lil was there, their conversation took on a different tone. They talked about wanting to go to the Breeze for drinks. Priscilla talked about her boat ride with Judy, teasing Judy about her rowing, and once again mimicking her. Trevor suggested they all go to Cafe Larke for lunch. Judy wanted to pop into Balthazar Books and browse.

"Great idea," Priscilla said. "Maybe Balthazar will have your latest book, Judy."

"Which, of course, you've already read," Jack said with a smirk.

Priscilla smiled. "Of course I have. Be nice, Jack."

Aunt Lil left to get more drinks and Ken muttered, "Yeah, be nice, Jack."

"Jack didn't mean any harm," Priscilla said, and I sensed from her tone of voice that she was referring back to their earlier conversation topic. From before Aunt Lil interrupted. "None of us do, Ken. We want to make sure you're doing all right. That's all. We want to know what's going on in your life. That's what friends are for."

Trevor was nodding eagerly. "Friends forever. Right?"

He looked at Jack, who smiled, showing his perfectly long, straight teeth. "Yeah, friends forever."

Priscilla reached across the table, opening a hand to Ken. An invitation to take it. Ken let out a long sigh. He pulled his chair back in. But he didn't take Priscilla's hand.

She said, "No secrets, Ken. We all agreed."

Ken snorted. "That's rich."

"You know what I mean."

"All right. No secrets, then. You want to know what's on my mind? I don't want to do this anymore. I don't want to meet every year. I don't want to do the phone calls and messages and check-ins."

"But, Ken..." Trevor stared at him, his eyes wide with horror. "You can't mean that. We're best friends. We stick together. Through thick and thin..."

"That's a marriage vow, Trevor," Ken said. "We're not married."

"We might as well be," Priscilla said. "Why should our

friendship be any different from a marriage? We took an oath, didn't we?"

"Our oath," Ken scoffed. "I'll tell you—"

Jack glanced over his shoulder at me.

He put a hand on Ken's arm and leaned close.

"Not the time or place to talk," he whispered.

Ken glanced back at me. And nodded at Jack.

Their conversation shifted again. Back to what fun things they'd do in Allington during their weeklong stay. A stiffly informal chat. Like something scripted. Now we were all playacting: I was pretending to enjoy the view, and they were pretending to talk about things they cared about.

Finally, I stepped away from the railing and headed inside, leaving them to their more intimate conversation. And leaving me to wonder what all the secrecy was about.

4

The *Allington Gazette* resided in a converted red-brick firehouse. Dad's click-clack typing rose to the tall ceilings, echoing in the cathedral-like space. Most of the desks, leftovers from the newspaper's heyday, stood empty on this Monday morning. Sometimes our irregular columnists joined us. But mostly it was just me and Dad, our desks facing each other.

Dad's click-clacking was loud. He was typing on a vintage typewriter. A manual typewriter sat on each desk at *The Gazette*.

This used to bug me.

Who used typewriters, anyway?

But once I came back to Allington, I came to appreciate Dad's quirky insistence that we type out first drafts on the old Underwoods and Remingtons and Royals. His own preference was for a teal green Olivetti Studio 44. Mine was a candy red Royal Quiet de Luxe.

But I wasn't typing. My laptop stood open next to the vintage typewriter, and I was busy searching online for information about Ken Tora and his friends. Lots of articles. After all, he was a well-known tech entrepreneur. He created the e-commerce app called *re:deem*, which had quickly become the most popular online marketplace for second-hand items. This part of the story was familiar: the app, his rise to fame, and the many millions he'd earned before he could even legally buy a drink.

But more recent articles suggested other big changes in his life. Ken had sold his remaining stake in *re:deem*. He'd stepped down as CEO. In an interview, he said he was withdrawing from the tech industry to focus on "spiritual matters." Maybe that was why he'd come to church yesterday. Maybe that was why he wanted to talk to Amy.

I searched online for articles related to Ken that mentioned his friends, Priscilla, Jack, Judy, and Trevor. I didn't have their last names, which made it more difficult. But by searching on Allington, I eventually found them.

Priscilla Nair was an actress, specializing in voice acting. She'd done the voices for several popular animated films. She'd also voiced audiobooks, from bestselling romance novels to classics by Jane Austen and the Brontë sisters. She lived in Seattle.

Jack Fox was an investment banker. He'd worked for a hedge fund. And he'd done something with cryptocurrencies. He lived in New York City.

Judy Budgie wrote murder mysteries featuring a clairvoyant woman who could talk not only to the dead but also to her cats. She wasn't a bestselling author, but she seemed to have a steady career. She lived in New Hampshire.

Trevor Jennings ran a comic book store in a small town in California. The only one to live in the same state as one of his friends: Ken also lived in California.

Apart from social media profiles and the occasional mention in a professional context, none of the others were as visible online as Ken. But that was to be expected. Ken was very, very visible.

Certainly nothing odd about the group of friends. Except their behavior yesterday. Which was suspicious. Or at least strange.

Then I remembered Gordon Groff.

I did a search on him. Nothing online. Only a listing for his gardening services. But when I searched *The Gazette*'s digital archive, I found a brief article mentioning Mr. Gordon Groff, a history teacher at Allington High, being dismissed.

"Hey, Dad. Do you remember Gordon Groff working as a high school teacher before he became a gardener?"

"Sure." Dad stopped typing. He leaned back in his chair, folding his arms across his ample belly. "He was fired because of some issue with a student. I can't remember the details. Something involving the police. Your mom will know."

"What about Ken Tora? What do you know about him?"

"Ken Tora...?" Dad pushed back his chair, rolling sideways from his desk and then toward me, so we could see each other better.

My dad was in his late 60s, heading toward 70. His full, white beard and fisherman sweater made him look like a jolly Hemingway impersonator.

He scratched his beard, thinking. "I know all the stuff about Ken becoming famous and making millions, of course. But there was something else. Something about him and his friends..."

He stared into the middle distance.

"That's it," he said, giving his belly a loud pat. "There was that case of the missing boy."

I sat up. "What missing boy?"

"Herman Hertz. A high school runaway. Packed his things and took off one day, leaving his family behind. Look it up. There should be something in *The Gazette*'s archives. I don't remember all the details, but I do remember this: they traced him to someplace by the Mexican border, then lost track of him. Obviously he'd left the country."

The story was ringing a bell. I would've been in college at the time. Undergrad. But a story like this—a missing high school kid was a big deal in Allington—would've made its way to me across the country. Yeah, I definitely remembered hearing about it back then.

"What's the connection with Ken Tora?"

"They were friends. Or at least they were part of a social group or something like it. Maybe it was a study group..." Dad scratched his neck, clearly trying to remember. "Anyway, Ken and his friends played a part in the search. I remember that. They were so determined to find their friend. Some of them even traveled across the country to track him down. We ran a story on it. As I said, the archives will have more details than I can remember."

I dove back into my computer, this time searching the online archive for any articles related to "Herman Hertz." I found several from 10 years ago. As I scanned them, I learned that Herman had come close to being kicked out of school. He had some trouble at home, too. But his parents expressed shock at discovering he'd run away. Despite his note to his parents being clear: he felt he didn't belong, wanted to make a life on his own terms, needed to get away.

Then I found an article where Herman's friends were interviewed. Ken and Jack. Ken described Herman as "a stand-up kind of guy." Jack said he believed he could convince Herman to come back, if only they could find him. "I'm going to look in every city across the country until I find him. I won't give up. I don't give up on my friends."

The Gazette article only featured Jack and Ken. There was a photo in the newspaper of them, slightly out of focus, and behind them stood the three other friends, younger versions of Priscilla, Judy, and Trevor.

The other articles focused on the family—the parents and Herman's brother—plus Herman's high school girlfriend. And then the police. Chief of Police Truby, my mom's predecessor and mentor, organized a search and coordinated with the state police. But after weeks had passed he said, "Based on our investigation, we're going to have to accept that Herman has left the country."

I went back to the article featuring Ken and Jack. What must such an experience do to a young person—a close friend running away like that? Disappearing from their lives. I'd be devastated. Maybe it wasn't so strange that the group of friends continued to stay in touch and meet year after year.

I shut down my browser. I'd spent far too much time on Ken Tora and his friends already. My deadline for a story was fast approaching—one on the upcoming annual town fair, with rides, food, and games. Plus, I had another in the works on new facilities at Allington's campgrounds.

I snapped my laptop closed and turned my chair and rested my fingers on the Royal typewriter. Here we go. Click-clack-clack.

Finishing both stories took the better part of the afternoon, and I'd just dropped the drafts onto Dad's desk when my sister Joy turned up.

She skipped down the long aisle of the firehouse.

All right, she didn't literally skip. But my sister Joy walks with a happy bounce to her step that's a second-cousin to a skip. Her yoga practice makes her light-footed. She practically dances through life. It ought to be annoying, but I could never entirely resist her happiness.

"Hey, Park," she said, giving me a bright smile.

I smiled, leaning back in my chair. "Hey, sis. What brings you to *The Gazette*?"

She held out an envelope. "Mail."

"Mail?" I took the envelope. It had no stamp. Only block letters saying,

FOR PARKER LEE AT THE ALLINGTON GAZETTE

"How did you get this?"

"I found it at the cafe," she said with a shrug. "Someone left it on the counter."

"I don't suppose you saw who left it?"

Joy shook her head. "Half of Allington came for lunch today. Ashley and I could barely keep up. Anyway, gotta go." She waved and turned on her heels. "Got a yoga class starting in 10 minutes."

She bounced down to the exit. Despite owning Cafe Larke, Allington's most popular cafe, and running our local yoga studio, Joy never seemed stressed. She was very zen. The yoga probably helped. But I believed it was in her bones—long before she discovered yoga, Joy had been Joy: chilled-out and happy.

So, who was leaving letters for me? I slipped a finger under the flap and tore open the envelope. Inside was a small sheet of paper. Lined. Folded up. The sender had written this:

10 years ago Herman Hertz disappeared. It's time he came home. Meet me on Gull Island at sunrise.

No signature. I turned over the piece of paper. Nothing else.

5

The black water splashed against the hull of the boat. I pulled on the oars one last time and the prow of the rowboat butted against a tree leaning over the dark lake.

I paused for a moment. A night bird cried somewhere in the distance, sending a little shiver down my neck. The sun would be up soon. Better get moving.

I threw a rope around the trunk and tied up the boat. Then hauled myself onto Gull Island.

Back on land, a few lights glowed in the windows of houses. Early birds. But much of Allington still slept, and the town, from the top of Chestnut Hill down to the docks, lay in darkness. Up above, a few stars still shone. I turned toward the woods. A glow was spreading above the hills and the mountains beyond.

Dawn. I was right on time.

I yawned. As a journalist, I learned to get up early. Especially if a story held promise. But when the alarm went off at 5 am this morning, it startled me so badly that I almost fell out of bed.

Now I pushed my way past low tree branches and through brambles, hurrying across the island. The note hadn't said where to meet. But Gull Island was small. And there was one logical place...

The trees parted, and I stepped into the clearing. Ahead of me lay the old cabin. It was a ruin. A storm had once blown off the roof and its top floor was exposed to the heavens. The entrance stood open, the door having fallen off its hinges.

Surrounded by trees, the clearing was dark. The cabin in shadow. In a little while, dawn's light would spread enough to brighten the island. But for now, I saw the scene half in darkness, half in memory, knowing where everything was.

I took a step forward and a soda can crackled underfoot.

Well, knowing where most things were...

Discarded cans and bottles littered the ground by the cabin. Other trash, too. Evidence of Gull Island's popularity as a hangout place for teens: easy to reach by rowboat or canoe, but still far enough from parents to be private.

As a kid, I'd spent many hours out here. Friends of mine used to call it "Snake Island," though no one ever actually saw a snake. Still, it lent the place an adventurous or even ominous quality.

I crossed the clearing. By the cabin, I peeked through the doorway. It was pitch black inside the cabin. Impossible to see anything.

"Hello?"

No answer. I blinked, hoping my eyes would adjust enough to the darkness for the interior to become clearer. I listened. Somewhere off to my left, something rustled in the undergrowth. Must be a bird.

No sounds from within the cabin. Should I go up the

stairs and through the trapdoor to the roof? I'd get a better view from up there.

I stared at the darkness within the cabin. Goosebumps prickled my arms, and I rubbed them. I wasn't usually afraid of the dark, but no way I was going inside.

I glanced over my shoulder. Dark trees all around. Was someone—whoever wanted to meet me—watching from a hiding place?

A knot twisted in my stomach. What if this wasn't a friendly invitation to talk? Going out here alone—maybe that wasn't so smart, after all. Dad had suggested I rope Scottie into coming along. But my brother wouldn't want to get up this early unless he'd be making money.

"No way I'm paying Scottie," I mumbled to myself. "I'm fine doing this on my own."

I was blabbing to myself. Yeah, I was clearly fine doing this on my own.

A loud snap. A twig. I thought of bones snapping and immediately pushed the idea away. Just a twig. Definitely just a twig.

"Hello?" I said again, this time to the dark trees. "Anyone there?"

Maybe the person was waiting for me on the other side of the cabin. I headed around the corner, walking as carefully as I could. Almost tiptoeing. Thinking of the reasons someone might be waiting back there yet not respond to my calls...

I slipped into a deeper darkness behind the cabin. Ahead of me, through the black trunks of trees, the charcoal-gray water moved.

My foot hit something hard. More trash? I kicked it again. No. Firm but soft. And it didn't budge. I blinked. It was big and long, like a big sack. I dug into my pocket and brought out my phone.

I should've used my phone earlier. A little light would help.

The screen lit up. I tapped the button for the flashlight.

The bright light flooded the space between the cabin and the trees, and I gasped. My heart flew into my throat and I stepped back.

A person was lying on the ground. No, not a person. Ken Tora. The back of his head a bloody mess.

I gripped my phone, my hand shaking, the beam of light wavering.

"Ken," I whispered.

But he couldn't hear me. He was dead.

6

"Are you sure you want to do this?" Mom asked.

We were on the back porch of the Lakeview Inn. She was wearing her police uniform. Neatly pressed, as usual. On her chest, the badge that said "Chief" shone. So did the brass name tag with "C. Lee" engraved. Both spotless. She was also wearing a concerned look.

I nodded. "I'm fine. Really. I want to hear what they have to say."

I wasn't fine. My body felt jittery, like I'd drunk a dozen cups of coffee. My heart kept beating too fast. My stomach felt airplane-turbulence wobbly. And whenever I closed my eyes I saw Ken Tora, the back of his head smashed in.

So I tried not to close my eyes.

Mom was about to go into the lounge at the Lakeview Inn. Deputy Douglas had gathered Ken's friends so Mom could talk to them. One of the perks of being the chief of police's daughter in a small town? She invited me along to crime scenes and interviews. Totally against police department protocol. But completely consistent with my family's procedures.

Mom said, "Nobody would blame you for needing to sit this one out."

"I'm fine. Fine-ish, anyway. And I want to know what happened out there. Was it Ken that sent me that note? Why? And who would want to kill him?"

Mom nodded. "I have the same questions. Let's go see what his friends say."

She opened the door to the lounge and we walked in.

Deputy Douglas, as baby-faced and nervous as ever, guarded the door that led to the inn's reception. Ken's friends had arranged themselves across the cozy lounge. Jack and Priscilla sat on an antique loveseat. Trevor on a nearby armchair. While Judy fidgeted in a corner between the fireplace and a triangular side table. On the table stood a heavy bust of Marie Antoinette, which she adjusted, turning it a little. Then changing her mind and turning it back.

"Judy," Jack said, "cut it out—you're driving me crazy."

Dark rings under his eyes. Heavy lidded. He looked sleep-deprived or hungover. He stifled a yawn.

Patricia put a hand on his knee. She spoke gently. "Leave her alone, Jack. She's upset. We're all upset. I mean, look at yourself."

"I'm tired," he said. "Dizzy. Must be coming down with something."

Priscilla moved her hand from his knee to his back and rubbed it gently.

Trevor was leaning forward with his elbows on his thighs and his chin in his hands, staring into space. A bug-eyed look of confusion on his face.

Jack ran a hand through his slick hair, smoothing it

back. Shaking off Priscilla. He stifled another yawn as he glared at my mom. A demanding look.

"So what are we doing here, chief?"

"We're talking about Ken."

"Don't you want to isolate us?" he said. "Talk to us individually?"

Mom cocked her head. "Why do you suggest that?"

He shrugged. "It's standard procedure, isn't it? For suspects."

"I didn't say you were suspects," Mom said.

I glanced at her. Jack was right, of course, and I wondered why Mom had chosen to gather them like this.

She added, "Right now, I'd like to understand what happened. When did you last see Ken?"

"Last night," Jack said. "We went for drinks at the Breeze. We must've left around 11 pm."

Mom nodded. "At 11:10 pm."

My brother Ray would've told her that. The Breeze belonged to him—him and his wife, Roxie—and even on a busy night, he had a pretty good idea of who came and went.

"Then what happened?" Mom asked.

"We came back here," Jack said. "Ken said he was tired and went to his room. I guess we all were. So we split up."

"You all went to your own rooms? Can anyone vouch for your presence during the night?"

Trevor shook his head. Judy crossed her arms and mumbled, "Not me..."

Jack hesitated. He glanced at Priscilla.

Priscilla said, "I didn't go back to my room. I stayed the night in Jack's room. So I can vouch for Jack."

Jack nodded. "And I can vouch for Priscilla."

Judy stopped fidgeting.

Trevor dropped his hands and straightened up, looking over. He stared at Priscilla. "You and Jack...?"

"I knew it," Judy said. "I knew you two were hiding something."

Priscilla smiled. A weak smile. Apologetic. "Yeah, we didn't want to make a big deal out of it. We started seeing each other a few weeks ago. I was thinking it might feel awkward if suddenly there was a couple in the middle of..."

Mom cut in: "In the middle of what, exactly? What is it that's kept you all together for so long?"

"Well—" Priscilla began, but Mom ignored her, turning to Trevor instead.

"I'd like to hear your take on it, Trevor."

Trevor stiffened. He rubbed the back of his neck.

"Uh, well..."

He glanced over at Jack and Priscilla. Jack nodded at him.

Trevor focused on my mom. "We're a study group."

"A study group? What do you study?"

"No, I mean we started out as a study group. In school. And then became friends. We called ourselves the Circle. Still do."

"And you still come back to Allington once a year?"

Priscilla said, "It's a reunion of friends. Is there anything strange about that?"

Mom shook her head. "Nothing strange, no. But years ago, something unusual happened to your group, didn't it?"

Silence. Something passed among the friends. A suppressed glance. An acknowledgement that no one needed to speak. But I felt it like a ripple through the room. After the silence had dragged on for a while, Priscilla finally broke it.

"Herman," she said. "He left us."

"To be precise," Mom said, "he disappeared."

"To be precise," Jack cut in, "Herman ran from Allington and went to Mexico—and from there, who knows where he went? Belize, maybe. We all looked for him. Heck, I even tracked him to a motel in a border town in Texas."

"He never contacted any of you?"

Jack shook his head. "No, but then why would he? Herman made it clear he wanted to start a new life." He frowned. "Why are we talking about Herman when it's Ken that's dead?"

Mom glanced at me. I knew she was thinking of the note I'd received.

"Right now, we need to understand the big picture," she said.

I watched her. She was studying Ken's friends—the Circle—one by one. This was why she wanted them together. She wanted to see how they interacted. Their dynamic.

"Well," Jack said, leaning back in the loveseat and crossing his arms, "I can tell you right now that no one here would ever want to hurt Ken."

Trevor nodded, looking miserable.

Judy didn't look up. She touched the Marie Antoinette bust again, then retracted her hand.

Priscilla glanced over at Jack, then dropped her gaze to the floor. "But someone did," she mumbled. "Someone did want to hurt Ken..."

7

"Anyone need more ale?" Ray called from the kitchen.

He came into the dining room with two growlers. Those big jugs for draft beer. For family dinners, he always brought beer from his brewery restaurant, the Breeze. Dad, his mouth full of food, gave Ray a thumbs up and Ray filled his pint glass. The froth flowed over the top.

"Oops," Ray said.

"Don't worry," Dad said. "Ancient tradition says it's good luck."

"You made that up," Amy said.

Dad smiled. "I'm ancient and it's my tradition."

"Dad joke!" Scottie and Joy chanted in unison, and we all laughed.

Ray left the growlers on a chair and sat down at the table. Roxie—his wife—had stayed home with Wimsey, their Dalmatian.

Joy was drinking sparkling water with a slice of lime. Mom and Amy had opted for a glass of red wine. Scottie was drinking a bottled beer. Not one of Ray's beers, but something obscure from Australia that he was considering importing. Another potential side hustle. I was drinking Ray's pale ale, and loving it, as usual. It managed to balance crisp and creamy, bitter and sweet, and it complemented the food perfectly.

Dad and Joy had made vegan shepherd's pie with mushrooms and root vegetables. Each one of us got a small, thick pie in one of Amy's many vintage ceramic pie dishes. She collected them. But she hadn't made the pie—she'd contributed with a big green salad.

Mom and Dad's stereo, which had an old-school turntable, played a vinyl record of Motown hits. The Supremes were singing: "*Set me free, why don't cha, baby? Let me be, why don't cha, baby?*"

We'd talked about the food and about the ale. As if we needed to do some throat clearing first. Now, we finally turned to the topic that everyone was curious about.

Scottie said, "So what's the deal with Ken Tora dying? I mean, seriously. This is bad for business."

"Scottie," Amy said, disapproving. "A man was killed."

Scottie shrugged. "I'm still right. Allington doesn't need another murder. Unless..." He put down his fork. "Unless we can somehow leverage the incident to our benefit. Aren't there true-crime murder tours? Isn't that a thing? And I mean, Allington has had its share of murders..."

Amy frowned. Deep disapproval.

Dad cut in: "Let's see what the investigation brings first, Scottie. Before you begin to monetize." He turned to Mom. "Any leads?"

"Too early," Mom said. "But of course we're looking at his friends."

"And the connection to Herman Hertz," I added. "The fact is that Ken—or someone else—wanted me to come to

Gull Island to learn something about Herman's disappearance."

"Why you?" Ray asked.

"Because I'm a journalist with *The Gazette*," I said.

"Yeah, but why the press? If the person wanted to reveal some big secret, why not go straight to Mom instead?"

Mom shrugged. "The person might be allergic to cops."

"Or the person is an avid reader of fine journalism," Dad said and winked at me.

"Joy," I said, still smiling at my dad's comment. "Pass me the salad, please."

Joy reached over the table, handing me the big bowl. I scooped up salad into my bowl. Meanwhile, thinking of Ken's body on Gull Island. Why would someone want to kill Ken? And who would want to do it? Someone from the Circle—his group of friends—or an outsider?

I remembered Ken going to church and then hurrying out when Jack turned up. But also something else: Judy getting upset when she saw Gordon Groff, the gardener. That was strange.

I mentioned it to the others.

"Gordon Groff," Mom said, nodding. "Glad you mentioned him. Because he's got a connection to the Circle."

"He does?"

"He used to be a schoolteacher. Taught high school history. But he was dismissed after a student accused him of stalking her."

I put down my fork. "Was it Judy?"

Mom nodded. "She reported seeing him outside her home. As did Priscilla. But it was when Groff got caught *inside* Judy's home—in her bedroom, in fact—that the hammer fell."

"Ugh," Joy said. "That's awful."

"Terrifying," Amy agreed.

Mom said, "So Groff was charged with breaking and entering, and he lost his job. He was unemployed for a while. Then became a gardener."

"And grumpy," I added.

"No," Dad said. "He was always grumpy."

"Funny coincidence that Groff happens to be at the inn when Judy and the others return for their reunion..."

Dad shrugged. "It might just be a coincidence. After all, Lil pays Groff to tend to her plants. He's got a legitimate reason to hang out at the Lakeview."

"Still," I said.

The record ended, and Dad got up to flip it over. Scottie groaned and complained for the umpteenth time about Dad insisting on using analog technology—when would he let Scottie install a wireless speaker with spatial audio so we could stream music from our phones? Dad flipped the vinyl, set down the needle, and Smokey Robinson's silky voice came on.

Meanwhile, Ray refilled his pint glass and asked me, "What did that note say?"

I knew it by heart by now. "*Ten years ago, Herman Hertz disappeared. It's time he came home.* That's all."

"I remember Herman," Ray said. "Years after Herman disappeared, his girlfriend and brother got together. Shirley and Manfred."

"You don't mean Shirley and Manfred at Big Heart Stationery?" I asked.

"Sure. It's a family business. Think about it: Big Heart. Big Hertz."

"Oh, I see. I never made the connection before."

Amy said, "Did the person mean literally 'come home'? Could it have been Herman himself who wrote it?"

"I don't think so," I said, spearing a tomato from my salad and eating it. "My money's on Ken. I can't be sure, but I think he wanted to meet me. And someone wanted to keep him from talking."

"But we don't have any evidence of that," Mom reminded me.

"No, I'm just speculating. Still, the whole disappearance thing smells fishy to me. Especially now that Ken is dead. Maybe Herman didn't leave to start a new life. Maybe he was running away from his friends. Or maybe—" I put down my fork. "—maybe Herman's dead. Maybe he was murdered before he reached Mexico."

Mom shook her head. "The investigation tracked him to the Mexican border."

"What if the investigation missed something?"

Mom frowned. "The investigation was closed."

"But what if—"

"It was closed," Mom said firmly. She glared at her shepherd's pie. "Closed."

I exchanged a glance with Dad. He shook his head. And we changed the subject.

What was eating Mom? She wasn't usually so reluctant to explore possibilities. But the Herman Hertz case seemed different. As if there was something personal about it.

8

The next morning, I spent my first couple of hours at *The Gazette* hammering out an article on my Royal typewriter about the death of Ken Tora, so we could include it in our Monday newsletter update. Once I'd done the draft and gotten Dad's feedback, I scanned it and revised it on my laptop, preparing it for publication.

Then I experienced a sudden need to buy a new notebook. I told Dad. He nodded, and with a twinkle in his eye, suggested that a notebook shortage was serious business—I'd better go to Big Heart Stationery right away.

"And while you're there, you might as well talk to Shirley and Manfred."

"Oh, good idea," I said with a grin, playing along. "I hadn't thought of that."

Big Heart Stationery lay halfway down Peony Lane, Allington's pedestrian shopping street. Locals and visitors alike love Peony. Flower boxes overflow with blooms. Umbrellas and awnings throw shade over benches. Colorful shops line the side of the meandering street as it winds its way up Chestnut Hill, the fanciest part of town.

I opened the door to the store, and a little bell jingled. Inside, the aisles of high-quality notebooks, pens, and greeting cards demanded my attention. At the back stood a counter. Behind that, an open door led to an office or storage room.

I browsed the shelves and racks. Most people have an Achilles' heel. A terrible weakness. I have two. Two heels, each a weakness: bookstores and stationery shops. God help me in a bookstore stocked with stationery.

I picked up a Moleskine notebook with a red cover. How many more half-finished notebooks could one woman own? I sighed. And put the notebook back down.

"Can I help you?"

Shirley Hertz approached me. Brown hair in a ponytail. Jeans and checkered shirt with the sleeves rolled up. She must be in her very early 20s. Young to be running a business. But sometimes that was the way with family businesses.

I said, "If I buy any more paper products, I'll run out of space in my bedroom. And my desk at *The Gazette* is already overflowing with stuff."

"I know you," she said. "You're Parker Lee. I follow your stuff in *The Gazette*. Plus, I read a couple of your articles when you worked for that big newspaper."

I smiled. "Then you read all my articles. I only got to write a few before I was laid off."

"And then you came back home."

"Yup. Then I came back home."

Right after I returned to Allington, everyone asked me about leaving the big city, and it made me feel so self-conscious. Even embarrassed. Like I'd failed. But now I saw how the universe had steered me in a positive direction. I loved Allington. I loved my family. I didn't want to go back to the city.

Shirley said, "And now you need a new notebook?"

"Actually, I need to talk to you. And to your husband."

"Oh?" She raised her eyebrows. "What's this about?"

I bit my lip. This was a delicate matter. Herman had disappeared 10 years ago. Shirley had married his brother. They ran a successful business together. On the surface, life was good. But I had no idea what kind of grief they still felt. No idea how much they missed Herman.

But sooner or later, I'd need to ask them.

I let out a breath. "It's about Herman."

Shirley stared at me. No widening of the eyes. No frown. Just a dead, empty stare. As dead as stone.

"Manfred," she called over her shoulder. "You'd better get out here."

A man lumbered out of the back room and went around the counter. He was linebacker big. But young. Freckles and sandy hair. He smiled at me, but quickly turned his attention to Shirley, putting a hand on her shoulder. A gentle touch.

"What's going on?"

"Parker here wants to talk about Herman."

He glanced at me. Lifted eyebrows. "Herman?"

"There's been—" I hesitated, looking for the right words. "—a development."

I told them about the anonymous message I'd received at *The Gazette*. Then about my discovery out on Gull Island.

"Ken Tora," Shirley said, her voice so low it was almost a whisper. "Killed? I can't believe it."

"And then there's the message mentioning Herman..." I said.

"But Herman ran away," Manfred said. "He left a note

that said he felt stuck and stifled, and our parents would never support his decisions to live the life he wanted to live. It was very clear. He wanted out."

"This note," I said. "Can you describe what it looked like? Was it obvious that Herman wrote it?"

Manfred shrugged. "It was Herman's handwriting."

"Wait," Shirley said. "Why do you ask about that?"

"Just making sure."

"But the police investigated," she persisted. "The case was closed."

"Given the anonymous message, I need to look into the possibility that something was overlooked."

Shirley frowned. "Are you saying the police will reopen the case?"

"No, no, I didn't say that. I'm the only one asking. Just a reporter from *The Gazette* looking into things."

Shirley's eyes shone. "When you went to journalism school and then got that gig at the big newspaper, I got so excited. I used to dream of becoming a Pulitzer prize-winning journalist. And here was a girl from my school becoming a big-time reporter."

"Well," I said, drawing out the word. "Hardly *big time*."

"And now you're back here," she continued, "doing investigative reporting to uncover what really happened to Herman."

"We know what happened," Manfred cut in. "He left us. He went to Mexico or Central America."

Shirley put a hand on Manfred's arm. "But what if that's not what happened?"

Manfred let out a long sigh. He stared at Shirley, a look that spoke of love and concern—but also weariness. He said, "You've dug into this before. Nothing's come of it. We've been over this so many times..."

"This time it's different," she said. "Ken Tora died. And it's got something to do with Herman."

"We don't know that."

Shirley turned to me. "But it seems like there's a connection."

I nodded. "I suspect there might be."

Shirley's face brightened. "See?"

"Yeah," Manfred said, frowning at me. "I see."

9

"I got the feeling Manfred would rather let sleeping dogs lie."

"Can you blame him?" Aunt Lil said, taking a sip of her nettle tea. "After so many years. So much uncertainty. If it were me, I'd prefer to believe the case was closed."

I shook my head. "Nah. You'd consult the stars—and they'd tell you to look again. To go deeper."

She smiled. "Yes, I might do that."

Aunt Lil and I were sitting on the back porch of the inn, eating lunch. Her chef had prepared a smoked salmon salad with sliced pears and a blue cheese vinaigrette. The sun glittered on her necklaces and bangles. A fresh breeze was blowing off the lake, caressing my face.

Aunt Lil had already finished her lunch. I speared the last pear on my plate and chewed it. It was a winning combination of sweet-and-tart pear with tangy blue cheese. Aunt Lil's chef was a miracle worker in the kitchen.

I filled Lil in on what else I'd learned. Then she cleared the table, bringing the plates and glasses inside. A moment later, she was back.

"Want to make the rounds with me? Or do you need to get back to *The Gazette*?"

"I'll walk with you for a while," I said.

Aunt Lil made the rounds several times a day, checking the inn's grounds, the dock, and then the rooms inside. Making sure everything was in tip-top shape.

She checked the crystals she'd placed on ledges to maintain a positive flow of energy at the inn. We moved down the steps toward the dock. She inspected the flower boxes along the porch railing, and sighed.

"Look how wilted they are. Groff was supposed to replace them."

I looked around. "Where is he?"

"He was meant to come again this morning, but the man has an uncanny talent for procrastination. Even when he's here. He seems to think his job as gardener includes fishing from my dock."

We walked out on the dock. Three rowboats stood tethered to the piles. For a small fee, guests could rent them. Sometimes Aunt Lil herself used them to get around. But usually there were four. The fourth was the one Ken had used.

Now she crouched down and undid one of the ropes and retied it.

"Guests rarely know how to tie up a boat."

She turned to another pile and frowned.

"Funny," she said. "I rented out one of the boats yesterday, not two."

"What's strange about that?"

She pointed out that, of the three boats, two had been improperly moored. With the discovery of Ken's body, she'd forgotten to check the boats at the end of the day yesterday. She redid the ropes on the second rowboat.

"Wait," I said. "Who did you rent the boat out to?"

"A couple from Italy. They rowed around yesterday afternoon. They left today."

"So someone else took out a rowboat yesterday?"

"Ken took one out, of course," Aunt Lil said. "That's why I'm down to three. Your mom's holding the fourth boat for forensics to examine."

I frowned. "Then who took this one?"

But we both guessed the answer. The killer. I looked up at the inn. The sun reflected on the windows. The trail from Gull Island led back to the Lakeview Inn.

10

That afternoon at *The Gazette*, Dad and I were concentrated on work. Silent. Though the firehouse wasn't exactly silent with the staccato click-clacking of our typewriters.

The click-clack was joined by the clip-clop of shoes echoing through the tall-ceilinged building. Mom came striding down the aisle between the desks.

Dad stopped typing and looked up. "A breakthrough in the case, honey?"

"No," she said. "Well, maybe."

Then stopped by my desk. She stared down at the red Moleskine journal on my desk.

I squirmed in my seat.

"All right," I said. "So I bought yet another notebook."

"Huh?"

She was clearly lost in her own thoughts. She wasn't thinking about my addiction to paper products. Or suspecting that I'd talked to Shirley and Manfred Hertz. So I didn't bother telling her I'd bought it out of guilt—feeling

I'd infringed on Shirley and Manfred's peaceful lives. Or more precisely, Manfred's life. Shirley seemed happy for me to infringe.

"Funny," Mom said. "It's a notebook like this one. Just black."

"Back up, Mom. You need to start at the beginning."

Dad chuckled. "In your mind, you told us the whole story. You just forgot we're not inside your mind."

"Sometimes it feels like you are," Mom said.

"Hey," Dad said. "Fifty years of knowing a person will do that."

"Fifty..." Mom smiled, cocking her head as she gave Dad a long look. "Gosh, we were so young back then."

"Oh, we're still young." Dad winked. "I'll show you tonight."

"Whoa, whoa." I waved my hands to get their attention. "You forgot you're not alone. Let's keep this conversation PG-rated, all right? Mom, what's this about a notebook?"

Mom straightened up, recovering her chief-of-police seriousness. "The thing is, we found a notebook among Ken's possessions."

"I love it when you say *possessions*," Dad said.

I groaned. "Can you two lovebirds give it a rest, please?"

Mom continued: "The notebook is like this one. A Moleskine. But it's with a black cover, not a red one."

"I know," I said. "I saw him writing in it. And reading over his entries."

Mom nodded. "Others have confirmed seeing him write in it. Would you say the notebook contained a lot of used-up pages?"

"A fair amount. Maybe as much as half the notebook. Why?"

"Because the notebook we found is blank. Every page intact. But simply blank."

I thought about that. Then shrugged. "If he's a big fan of notebooks and he was staying in Allington for a week, maybe he brought a spare. Why does it matter?"

"It matters because the paper in the notebook matches the message you received."

I sat up. "I knew it. It was Ken. He sent me the message."

"Very likely," Mom said. "But this notebook is intact. No pages are missing. And you said yourself you saw him writing a lot in his notebook."

"So if he ripped out a page, it was from the notebook I saw. The one he was actively writing in. The one that's missing."

I leaned back in my chair, crossing my arms. Staring into space. I pictured Ken ripping a page out of his notebook to write the anonymous message, slip it into an envelope, and then leave it on the counter at Cafe Larke. Counting on Joy to find it and bring it to me.

It seemed like an impulsive action. Like someone desperate to talk.

But why send an anonymous note? Why ask me to meet on Gull Island at dawn? Why not just show up at *The Gazette* and have a private conversation here?

Again, I pictured Ken ripping out that page. Surreptitiously writing a message. Slipping it into an envelope and leaving it on the counter at Cafe Larke.

Another image came to me: Jack standing in the entrance to Shepherd's Gate Church, waiting for Ken. Intercepting him?

And then another image: Gordon Groff sitting on the Lakeview Inn's dock, just below the porch where Ken was sitting. Lurking.

Did Ken send me the anonymous message because he was being watched? Because he was afraid someone would find out?

11

At the end of the day, I dropped by Cafe Larke to grab a cup of tea and chat with Joy. Cafe Larke is a cozy cafe on the corner of Main Street and Peony Lane. Inside, cheerful colors brighten its walls, and framed prints showcase paintings by Allington's famous impressionist painter, Julia Larke. Joy loves Larke's art, which is why she named the cafe in her honor.

While I sat a table, flicking through a magazine, and waiting for Joy to take a break from work to talk to me, I spotted Mom. She came into the cafe. For a moment, I thought she was coming in to say hi to me or to Joy. She had that determined look she got when she wanted to zero in on a person.

But Mom made a beeline for another table.

The gray-haired woman sitting there looked up. She'd been sipping from a cup of coffee. Now she put the cup down.

"Charlene," the woman said.

"Tamara," Mom said. "Mind if I join you?"

The woman gestured at the other chair at the table, but

she seemed reluctant, displeased that Mom was interrupting.

Tamara...

The woman looked vaguely familiar.

Tamara...

Then I remembered. Tamara Truby. Tom Truby's wife.
Tom Truby had been the chief of police before mom
assumed the role. Usually, this wouldn't make me interested.
But Chief Truby headed up the investigation into Herman
Hertz's disappearance. Could this be why mom wanted to
talk to his wife?

It was a long shot, but I was eager to know what they
would say.

Now that they were seated together, the music and the
chatter of other customers made it hard to hear what they
said. So I grabbed my mug of tea and moved to a stool by
the window, which was closer to them. I pretended to be
engrossed in my magazine. Turning the pages slowly as I
eavesdropped.

"...he's got good days and bad."

"I'd still like to visit and say hi. Maybe he'd enjoy some
company."

"He's got company."

"Of course," Mom said, her voice soft. "And you do so
much for him. You're not just his wife. You've become his
primary care giver. It must be a lot."

"Someone needs to do it."

"I could help."

"Tom gets exhausted easily. So we keep excitement to a
minimum. Lots of people trudging in and out of our house
—it isn't good for him."

"I'm not lots of people, Tammy. I'm more than that."

Tamara grimaced. She took a sip of her coffee.

"I'll give it some thought, Charlene. But he needs peace and quiet."

"I understand. Still, I'd like to talk to him."

Tamara stiffened. She frowned. "I knew it. You want to talk about work. Police stuff. I told you, he can't get excited. It's bad for him."

"Tammy..." Mom said, a note of pleading in her voice. Mom never begged people for anything. It made me listen even harder, wondering what in the world could be so important.

"Hey, Park," Joy said, interrupting. She slipped onto the stool next to mine. "Sorry, I took so long. Ashley's got everything under control now, but who would've thought we'd get so many customers on a Wednesday afternoon?"

I tried to talk to Joy while also eavesdropping on Tamara and Mom, but Joy's bubbly energy eclipsed the quiet conversation behind me. And suddenly, the scrape of a chair ended things. Tamara got to her feet.

She said, "I said I'd think about it. Now, please, leave us alone."

She strode out of the cafe. Mom swiveled on her chair to gaze after her. She caught me and Joy looking and quickly turned back around. As if embarrassed by the whole thing. Which wasn't like Mom at all.

12

When I dropped by the Lakeview Inn the next morning, Gordon Groff was sitting on the dock again with a fishing pole in his hand. His face caved into a deep frown. Glaring at the water below his feet as if the fish had insulted him.

As I stepped out onto the dock, he didn't lift his gaze. But he said, "Unless you've got business here, don't go scaring the fish off."

"You heard about Ken Tora?"

A one-shoulder shrug. "Yeah. Who hasn't?"

"But you knew him."

"He was in *Time Magazine*. Who didn't know him?"

"You used to be his teacher."

Groff tugged at the fishing pole. The line tightened. Then went slack. He continued to glare at the water, ignoring my statement.

I said, "Did you know Ken and his friends would be visiting Allington this week?"

He didn't answer. It was as if he'd blocked me out, pretending I didn't exist.

"Mr. Groff," I said. "The police will want to know the answers to these questions, too."

"Then let them ask."

"But—"

"You journalists have done enough damage already. Leave me alone."

I stared at him. My mouth was open. I closed it and turned, heading back up the steps. Was he referring to the scandal some years ago that got him fired from his teaching job? He could hardly accuse *The Gazette* of a witch hunt. I'd read the articles in our archives. They were straightforward reports about Groff being accused of stalking Judy and Priscilla, and then the cops catching him red-handed in Judy's bedroom. His name wasn't even mentioned in most— he was simply "the teacher." But bitterness about the past could so easily rewrite history—Groff might prefer to blame my dad and the paper than blame himself for what happened.

Getting to the top of the steps, lost in thought, I nearly bumped into someone.

"Whoa. Almost knocked me down."

I looked up. Jack grinned at me. As before, he'd slicked back his hair. He wore khakis and a button-down shirt. Loafers. The uniform of the young conservative. And to complete the picture, he'd tucked a copy of *The Wall Street Journal* under his right arm.

"I'm glad to see you," I said.

"Oh?" His smile broadened, and he gave me a once-over look, checking me out. It made the little hairs on my neck stand up. "Then I'm glad to see you, too."

"I want to ask you about Ken."

His smile faltered. Fell into a frown. "Of course you do."

"You showed up at Shepherd's Gate Church the other day."

"No crime against attending church, is there?"

"I got the feeling you were picking up Ken. Like an escort. Like you didn't want him to talk to the pastor."

Jack laughed. "An escort? Are you calling me a male escort? I must look a certain way. Handsome. Now I'm flattered."

A bad joke. He was deflecting. So I pressed on. "Ken didn't expect you, did he?"

Jack shrugged. "I was bored. I knew he was going to church, so I went to see what it was all about."

"Did Ken tell you he was going?"

Jack put a finger to his lips. A pensive look. "You know, he must have. Or he told someone else, and they told me. Either way, I knew he was going, and it turned out that he was there."

Slippery. It was as if Jack was performing. Dancing around the topic. And enjoying it.

"Look, Jack—" I said.

"What's going on?" Priscilla and Judy emerged from the inn, and Priscilla came to stand by Jack's side, linking arms with him. She smiled. "Jack?"

"Oh, just chatting," Jack said, the picture of innocence.

Her eyebrows curled into a frown. She looked from Jack to me.

I said, "I was simply wondering—"

But a yell from below us interrupted me. I turned. Down on the dock, Groff was hauling in his line. The fishing rod bent dangerously low toward the water. Something heavy on the end. He grabbed the line, apparently to spare his rod, and heaved an object to the surface. A handle. A shaft. Then the flat blade.

"A shovel…" I muttered.

Groff threw it onto the dock, and it clattered loudly. The lake water splashed at his feet.

"That's the shovel," he said. "The one that went missing."

He glared up at me and Jack as if we were to blame. Judy, flinching under his gaze, took a step back. Priscilla glanced at Jack.

No longer smiling, Jack looked thoughtful. Then shrugged and said, "A spade is a spade."

"You—" Groff jabbed a finger in Jack's direction. "—you did this."

Jack laughed. "Right. I stole a shovel and threw it in the lake to ruin your fishing. Don't be ridiculous. Come on, ladies."

He put his arms around Priscilla and Judy and led them toward the door to the inn. Groff continued to stare up, his eyes lit with anger. But with the others gone, his gaze fell on me.

"I know what I know," he growled.

"And what is that?" I asked.

He spun around, turning his back on me. Refusing to answer.

What did he know? And was he right—had Jack stolen a shovel and then thrown it in the lake? I couldn't think of a reason anyone would do that.

13

A van from a TV station stood parked outside the Lakeview Inn when I left for *The Gazette*. A woman spoke to a cameraman about the exterior shots of the inn they needed. I overheard her say, "And then we can look for that missing kid's house afterward."

I hurried away before the TV journalist got the idea to talk to me. I wasn't surprised the media was turning up. Ken Tora's death by foul play would be juicy, sensational news. More vans would probably turn up soon, and for a day or two, Allington would play host to press from around the country. Then they'd move on. The media had the attention span of a goldfish.

But the news presenter's idea to reference Herman Hertz's disappearance reminded me of my own to-do this morning: dig into the file archives at *The Gazette*.

When I got to the old firehouse, Dad was already busy clack-clacking away at his typewriter. He smiled when I got to my desk. Then took the opportunity to get up and go to our kitchenette to put on the kettle for another cup of coffee. We had a drip coffee maker and a stovetop espresso pot, but Dad preferred a classic porcelain pour-over.

The water boiled, and he poured it onto the grounds in the filter. The coffee trickled into his mug. Such a gratifying sound.

"So, what's new?" he asked.

I told him about Groff fishing out a shovel.

"I called Mom," I said. "Though it might have nothing to do with the case."

"Might not," Dad agreed. "Then again, it might. Coffee?"

I thanked dad, and with a cup of black coffee, sat down at my desk. I booted my computer and then logged onto our archival database. We had filing cabinets along the walls, but a few years ago, Dad finally got around to digitizing everything. It was a lot quicker to find an old article on the computer than rifling through the filing cabinets. Dad, of course, preferred the old way of finding information.

A search for "Herman Hertz" turned up a long list of articles. I clicked the first one and began to read.

There were a couple of articles related to school events that had nothing to do with his disappearance. But soon I got to stories about the kid running away and his friends and family trying to track him down.

Initially, it seemed, the police were reluctant to get involved, and there was a reader's letter to the paper complaining about Chief Truby's lack of action. Pressure must've mounted, because an article a month later contained a quote by Truby saying the Allington Police Department was doing what it could to help the family track down Herman.

Another couple of months later, *The Gazette* ran a full-page story about the disappearance and the friends who refused to give up. A photograph showed Jack, Trevor, Ken,

Priscilla, and Judy, and the caption described them as a "study group turned amateur sleuths—five friends determined to track down their friend."

They traced Herman's journey from Allington via bus from town to town. *The Gazette*—it was my dad writing—couldn't verify this investigation, because the friends had spoken with bus company employees who'd since moved on, and since Herman presumably paid in cash, he wouldn't be easy to trace. Until he came to a border town. There he stayed at a motel—the Amistad—before apparently crossing the border into Mexico. Then the friends lost track of him. Jack was quoted as saying that, "We're working together to find Herman. I know Herman's out there—and as long as I know that, I won't give up looking. None of us will."

Was that why they continued to meet once a year? Not just a happy reunion of best friends, but a way to keep the search alive? Or simply to keep the memory alive?

I read another half a dozen articles, then came back to the one with Jack's quote. The border-town motel was mentioned. It seemed like a long shot. By now, the place was probably no longer in business. But I gave it a try and searched for it online.

And there it was. Motel Amistad. I called the number.

"Amistad, whaddya want?" a raspy-voiced woman barked.

"I'm trying to track down a person who stayed with you about 10 years ago."

Audible sigh. "Honey, ain't about Herman Hertz, is it?"

I gripped my phone tighter. "Yes, actually it is."

"Like I told the other person who called, we keep records. A whole heap of records. My husband's a hoarder. Doesn't like to throw anything out. It's killing me."

"So Herman stayed at your motel? For how long?"

"One night. That was it. Then he checked out and left."

"You don't happen to remember him, do you?"

A deep, throaty laugh. "You serious? You think I remember every Tom, Dick, and Harry who comes through here?"

"Of course not..."

"Like I told the other person who called, all I've got is an old registration book covered in dust and food stains. Pretty gross, actually. And it says Herman Hertz stayed here. But I mean it could be a different Herman Hertz. It's not like we checked his ID or anything."

"Wait," I said. "You mean you didn't ask for a driver's license or other ID? Aren't you supposed to?"

"Honey, I know we're supposed to. But with everyone coming and going, a kid stays one night, pays cash, and then moves on—it's no big deal."

I took a sip of coffee, considering that. It was a big deal for the investigation. Pretty inconvenient if you were trying to track someone.

"I don't have all day," the woman said. "You want anything else?"

"Yes, please. Can you tell me who the other person was? The one who called before me?"

"Sherry," the woman said. "Nah, that's not right."

My heart beat faster. "Shirley?"

"Bingo. Shirley. Guess you know her, huh?"

I sure did.

14

The little bell over the door jingled as I stepped into Big Heart Stationery. My mission was to find Shirley and talk to her, but as soon as I laid eyes on the notebooks—and oh, a set of ballpoint pens in bold reds, oranges, and yellows—I got distracted. A display table held Julia Larke-themed items: wire-bound calendars, envelopes, and even erasers with prints and patterns taken from Larke's impressionist paintings.

"Can I help you?" Manfred asked, and I jumped a little. I hadn't heard him approach.

"I'm doing my best to resist everything in your store."

"I can't help you. I'm addicted to paper products, too."

"Plus, you sell them."

He smiled. "There's that, too." He cocked his head, looking at me. "But you didn't come to buy more notebooks, did you?"

I shook my head.

He sighed. "You came to ask me more questions about Herman."

"Actually, I had a question for Shirley."

"Shirley's out. But maybe I can help. There are no secrets between Shirley and me."

I glanced around the store. No other customers. And no sign of Shirley. Should I wait for her to come back? But then Manfred might reveal something Shirley would be reluctant to share.

"Shirley called the motel Herman stayed at."

He put a hand to the back of his neck and slowly shook his head. "Shirley," he whispered, as if he was talking to her, not me. It made me wonder if this wasn't the first time she'd done such a thing.

I said, "She's contacted the motel before."

"Long time ago, yes. But there was a time when she spent much of her time digging in newspaper archives. She contacted the remaining members of the Circle—Herman's old friends—to ask them questions. She even cornered them when they came back for their reunion."

"How did they react?"

He shrugged. "Some were understanding. Others stand-offish. I don't blame them. Herman left us a long time ago, and we're all trying to move on with our lives."

"You're sure he left you?"

He gave me a weary look. "Chief Truby confirmed it, and I've chosen to believe it. The alternative is that I spend the rest of my life in anguish about what happened to my brother. I've chosen to let go. To move on. I just wish Shirley would, too."

"She hasn't given up?"

"I thought she had. But if what you say is true, I was wrong."

He picked up a pencil sharpener shaped like a heart. He turned it over in his hand, examining it as if it were a precious stone. Then placed it back on the display table. Gently.

"Herman was a smart kid. But troubled. Restless. Was I upset when he ran away? You bet. But I wasn't surprised."

"What was his relationship with his friends like?"

"The Circle? They were a study group. All kids from the wrong side of the tracks, if you know what I mean. But they helped each other excel. And excel way beyond expectations. Look at the colleges they went to: Stanford, Princeton, Yale, Columbia. Only Trevor went to a state college. And they're almost all hugely successful."

"You think they were successful because of how they helped each other?"

He shrugged. "I think it was part of it, yeah."

I checked the time. I had to go. I said, "Thanks for talking to me, Manfred."

"I hope you know what you're doing, digging up the past like this."

"I'm just looking for answers."

He nodded. "That's what Shirley would say. But what if you find more questions? What if you dig up more pain? Tell me..." He looked me in the eye. Unflinching. And deep within his gaze, I saw a deep sorrow. "Will it be worth it?"

15

At the Breeze that night, I spotted Jack and Priscilla sitting in a booth, side by side. Across from them sat Trevor. The three of them were having drinks. Priscilla nudged Jack, and he laughed. But Trevor didn't look happy. He was playing with a napkin, picking it apart until it was a little pile of shreds.

"Shirley Hertz?" Aunt Lil said, bringing me back to our conversation. "What's she up to?"

I shook my head, turning around again to face the bar. I slurped the foam off my pint of cream ale. I'd gone to the Breeze to have a drink, and found Aunt Lil waiting there, as if we'd agreed to meet. She said her tea leaves told her I'd be coming to the Breeze tonight.

My brother Ray was behind the counter wiping off beer glasses and hanging them from the overhead rack. He was listening to our conversation, occasionally commenting.

Now he said, "So Shirley's looking into Herman's disappearance again? Maybe that's not a bad thing."

"Another sleuth on the case," Aunt Lil said. "Wonderful. But it doesn't sound like you learned much. Either of you."

"I don't know about that," I said.

I thought again about what the woman at the motel had told me. What it added up to. At first, learning that Shirley had called before me made me focus all my attention on her. But later, going back over Herman's stay at the motel, something the woman had said kept bothering me, like an itch that refused to go away.

I said, "The woman at the motel says Herman stayed with them. But she's basing this on an old registration book that has his name in it, and it shows he paid cash. She admits they probably didn't check his ID. For a single night paid in cash, they wouldn't bother."

Aunt Lil looked at me.

Ray had stopped wiping his beer glass. He frowned. "What're you saying, sis?"

At that moment, Jack stepped up to the bar and ordered another round. Ray got busy making drinks: a glass of white wine for Priscilla and beers for Trevor and Jack.

"So this is where the cool kids hang out," Jack said with a smile. More like a sneer.

I cocked my head, looking at him. "Jack, when you went to the Amistad to find Herman, did they provide you with any proof he'd stayed there?"

Jack's smile didn't falter. But maybe I was mistaken—I thought his eyes narrowed slightly. He said, "Herman? Look, I understand that with Ken's death you'll dig up the past. But don't forget you're opening old wounds—and for what? A few more readers for your local paper?"

Inwardly, I flinched.

I was doing my job. Sometimes journalists had to open old wounds to find answers. But part of me shrank at his accusation. Part of me felt he was right.

But I kept staring at him. Waiting for an answer. Trying not to show my doubt.

He ran a hand over his hair, making sure it was slicked back. Then he sighed. "All right, if you absolutely need to know. They showed me a registration book. And the staff remembered him. Young kid traveling alone. Heading to Mexico. One of them noticed how unusual it was."

"Do you remember who that staff member was?"

He shrugged. "I don't. It was a long time ago. My focus was on finding Herman, not keeping track of who I talked to. But the police did a report. Why don't you ask your mom?"

Ray placed the three drinks in front of Jack, and Jack threw down a couple of twenties.

"Keep the change," he said, grabbed the drinks. He turned away, but then stopped, glancing over his shoulder at me. "Don't think for a second Herman's old friends don't still feel the pain. We do. Why do you think we keep meeting every year?"

I watched him cross the floor, returning to the booth. So did Aunt Lil and Ray.

Ray leaned across the bar and dropped his voice.

"That sounded earnest, but honestly, there's something fishy about that guy..."

"Deep-sea fishy," I agreed.

"He's an Aries," Aunt Lil said, as if that explained everything.

I added, "Jack's explanation about talking to motel staff —that'll be hard to prove. There's actually no proof Herman stayed there."

"But someone did," Ray said. "Someone checked in and paid cash."

"Right. Someone. But we can't be sure it was Herman."

I glanced back over my shoulder toward the booth. Jack was laughing. Priscilla smiled. Trevor drank his beer, looking miserable. Somehow Jack was mixed up in Herman's disappearance. I was sure of it.

Ray filled a pint glass with beer for a customer. "So, you're saying that Herman may never have reached the Mexican border."

"I'm saying he may never have left Allington."

Ray blew out a breath. "Holy moly, Park. That's serious. Do you know what you're saying? I mean, Chief Truby closed the case years ago."

I nodded. I didn't like it any more than Ray did. But I couldn't ignore the facts: Herman's stay at the Amistad might be a fiction. And why would somehow impersonate Herman to create a trail leading to the Mexican border? The answer was chillingly obvious: because they didn't want the authorities to keep looking for Herman. And the authorities had, in fact, stopped looking.

The question was why the police hadn't uncovered the lie in the first place.

"I know what I'm saying, Ray. I'm saying the Allington Police Department may have bungled the investigation."

Aunt Lil's jewelry rattled as she gave a dramatic shudder. "Oh, that's not good. Charlie won't like that."

Ray grimaced. "Yeah, what about Mom? Where does she fit into all this?"

"Yeah," I said, my heart sinking like a stone. "Mom."

16

One benefit of moving back into Broadstairs House, my childhood home, was dinner with my family. At least once a week, often on Sundays, we had a big family dinner in the dining room. But most nights, it was just the five Lee family members living at Broadstairs who ate in the kitchen: Mom, Dad, Joy, Scottie, and me.

Usually, it was a delight. Music on the stereo. Lively chatter. Tonight, though, I didn't take any pleasure in sitting down to the meal.

How was I going to talk to Mom about the Herman Hertz investigation? I had to find a discreet way to bring up the Amistad and what I'd learned. Maybe over dessert. Or after dinner, while doing dishes...

I glanced over at her. She'd changed out of her police uniform and wore a t-shirt and jeans. Casual. She was scooping salad onto her plate while she listened to Scottie talk about a new t-shirt design he was sure tourists would go crazy for. Dad was quizzing Joy about her plans for Cafe

Larke during the summer—the specials, poetry readings, and an expanded kids corner.

I kept quiet, slouching in my chair. Playing with my food. I separated tomatoes from lettuce. I organized my pasta into a square.

Joy nudged me. "Hey, kid. What's on your mind?"

I stiffened. Then straightened up and speared a piece of pasta and shoved it in my mouth. "Nothing, really."

"Which is another way of saying 'a lot.'" Joy put a hand on my shoulder. "Tell me."

Joy had this incredible skill: she could touch you and say a few words, and it would loosen something inside, making it almost impossible not to open up. She would've made a great minister. But I guess Amy got there first.

I took a deep breath and let out a long sigh. And realized that Joy wasn't the only one looking at me. Dad was, too. And Scottie had stopped talking. Mom raised her eyebrows.

"Go ahead, Park," she said. "Tell us."

Oh, great. So much for finding a discreet way of talking to Mom about the investigation.

"Uhm..."

"Is this about Ken Tora's death?"

"Kinda..."

Dad said, "Park's been doing some research on Herman Hertz and his disappearance."

Mom nodded. "I guess that makes sense. It must be what's kept that group of friends together all these years. The trauma."

"Well," I said. "It's more than research..."

Scottie served himself another helping of pasta. "Oh, come on, Park. Spit it out."

"You can tell us," Joy said encouragingly.

I knew I could tell them, of course. But could I tell Mom?

I sighed. Nodded.

"See, I tried to piece together what happened to Herman. So I looked at the old articles. And I contacted the motel he stayed at before crossing into Mexico. Or I should say, I contacted the motel that had a registration book with his name in it."

Mom frowned. "You make it sound as if there's some doubt."

"There is—" I swallowed. "—some doubt."

Dad said, "It's all right, Park. Go ahead and tell us." He gave Mom a look. Her frown didn't ease up, but she nodded, as if to say, "Go ahead."

So I told them about my call with the woman at the motel, and how she'd made it clear that Herman's name appeared in the old registration book, but that all she could confirm was that he'd paid in cash and that they wouldn't have checked his ID.

"It was apparently difficult to track Herman after he left Allington. The motel is the only proof that he came near the Mexican border. Or that he even left town."

"Of course he left town," Mom said.

I filled them in on what Jack had said—that he'd confirmed with motel staff that Herman had stayed there, but that he hadn't kept track of who he'd talked to. That Herman's stay couldn't be corroborated today. That it seemed to be based on hearsay.

"So the person who stayed the night at the motel could've been Herman Hertz," I said. Then paused. "Or it could've been someone else."

"It must've been Herman," Mom insisted. "Chief Truby's investigation confirmed it. I read the report myself. It cited the motel staff who'd seen the kid. Chief Truby closed the case," Mom concluded with a sharpness to her voice. A warning to back off.

"I know," I said softly. Trying to show I wasn't angling for a fight. "But what if Chief Truby missed something? What if he took the information at face value and didn't look deeper? What if he was meant to believe Herman stayed at the motel?"

A screech. Mom's chair scraping against the hardwood floor. She stood up.

"Chief Truby didn't cut corners."

"I'm not saying he did. I'm—"

She folded her napkin and placed it on her plate.

"Thanks for dinner," she mumbled, then strode out of the room.

I gaped at her back. She turned the corner into the dining room and disappeared.

"What the heck...?" Scottie said, as surprised as I was.

Joy looked worried. "She never gets this upset."

It was true. Usually, Mom could face a steady onslaught of slings and arrows without flinching. She was strong. Stoic. She didn't walk away from conflict.

"It's Chief Truby," Dad said with a sigh. "Her mentor. He was like a father to her."

"But everyone makes mistakes," I said. "Mom would be the first to admit that."

"It's not about that. Truby's sick. He's dying. Questioning how he handled the Hertz investigation—"

"It's bad timing," I said, understanding.

Dad nodded.

I got to my feet. Dropped my napkin on my plate. I couldn't let this fester.

Mom was sitting outside on our porch swing. Staring out at the dark lake. Above the waters, above the woods and the hills and mountains beyond, the first stars of the evening twinkled.

I sat down next to her. I thought of all the things I could say to her. But in the end, none of the words would make much of a difference. So I slipped an arm around her. For a while, she sat rigid next to me. Then she leaned into me, and our heads touched.

Together, we looked out at the night. No words exchanged. Just the warmth of our bodies together.

After a while, Mom straightened up and ran her hands across her cheeks, wiping away tears.

"Do you have plans tomorrow?" she asked me.

The question surprised me. I shrugged.

"Good," she said. "Because we have work to do."

17

The Trubys—Tom and Tamara—lived halfway around Lake Allington. A dirt road through the woods went past the few cabins nestled among the trees, each one with a stunning view of the water. A dense canopy cast shadows over the cabin. Especially since the morning sun still hung low.

Allington was no metropolis, but out here, it felt so much more peaceful. I took a deep, deep breath. The air seemed cooler and cleaner, too.

Mom parked the police cruiser in their driveway, just off the dirt road. A staircase made of rough-hewn rocks led us down the steep slope to the log cabin. Our feet disturbing pine cones, which tumbled down ahead of us. Brittle twigs snapping.

A wood sign, carved and painted, dangled from chains outside the front door. A single word on the front: "Welcome."

Beyond the cabin, I glimpsed a dock.

Halfway down the stairs, the screen door inside opened,

then the front door, and a woman appeared on the step. The one I'd seen at Cafe Larke. She had short, gray hair. She wore a white shirt and a pair of khaki cargo pants. Arms crossed over her chest. A slight frown on her face.

"Tamara," Mom said.

"Charlene."

She didn't speak my mom's name with any joy. There was something guarded about her, like we were door-to-door sales people about press her into an annual subscription she didn't want.

Reaching the doorway, Mom put out a hand and grasped Tamara's arm. "I'm so glad to see you again. Thank you for having us."

"Like I told you on the phone, and like I told you at Cafe Larke, this isn't a good time."

"I understand." Mom glanced up at the welcome sign. Then back at Tamara. "And I appreciate it."

Not taking no for an answer. It wasn't lost on Tamara. She grimaced. Then turned and walked into the house, apparently expecting us to follow. Mom jerked her head. A gesture for me to come inside.

The cabin was dark. There was the musty smell of wet wood. And a smell I associate with oldness: talcum powder and something medicinal. Astringent. Melancholy.

"Today isn't one of his better days..." Tamara muttered.

"We won't take much of his time," Mom said.

We passed a kitchen on our left with a wooden counter. A round kitchen table in a nook straight ahead. A living room opening up to the right with a screen door leading to a porch. Tamara headed toward the door and pulled it open.

Out on the porch, the first thing I saw was the breath-taking view. Allington, with its docks and houses on the far side, Chestnut Hill lifting the town toward the sky. Gull Island, looking like a cluster of trees rising straight out of the lake. And everywhere else: water and woods. From this angle, the Lake Allington Resort & Spa remained hidden somewhere off to the left.

But as Tamara and Mom walked down the porch, my attention shifted.

A man sat in a rocker on the deck. He was facing the lake, staring into the distance. I stopped, frozen.

Tom Truby, the chief of police of my childhood, had once been of medium height and all shoulders. As solid as rock. Meaty. He'd walked into a room or into a fraught situation, and it would make people take a step back, calm down, or even turn and run. He had that kind of commanding presence.

Now he was half his original size. His cheeks had deep hollows. His skin, which I remembered as tan, had turned a pasty gray, and his skull and bones pressed outward. As if they were trying to escape.

"Tom," Mom said, her voice low.

He turned. Impossibly slowly. When he saw her, the hint of a smile appeared on his cracked lips.

"Charlie," he said in a whispery rasp. He nodded. "Good to—" He caught his breath. Every word cost him. "—see you."

Mom looked around. There was only one other chair on the deck. Tamara went to the chair and sat down. Claiming it. A sign that she didn't want us to get too comfortable.

Mom didn't say anything. She simply crouched down next to Tom and took his hand. "How are you, old friend?"

Tom licked his cracked lips. His tongue was the color of his skin. No saliva wetted his lips. He said, "Dying, Charlie. I'm dying."

Mom nodded.

Tom sighed and closed his eyes.

"That's enough," Tamara snapped. "Can't you see how tired he is? He needs to rest. To conserve his energy."

"I wouldn't disturb you—" Mom said, looking at Tamara and then back at Tom, including both of them. "—if it wasn't important. And urgent."

Tom opened his eyes. "Important. And urgent. That's when you take immediate action. I taught you that."

"Yes, how to prioritize. Is it important? Yes. Is it urgent? Yes."

"The murder," Tom croaked. "Ken Taro."

"You heard."

Tom nodded.

"Then you can guess what I'm going to ask you about?"

Again, Tom nodded. Mom was silent for a moment. Then Tom said, "Herman Hertz."

The scrape of a chair. Tamara had shot to her feet. "Not that again, Tom. You know how upset you get talking about old cases."

Tom raised a hand. Slowly. Fingers splayed a little. "Please," he said, his voice so thin and worn it was barely audible. "My love. I need..." He coughed. His whole body crumbling under the effort of coughing. When he recovered, he said, "I need to close this..."

"But you closed the case," Tamara said. "It's history."

Tom shook his head. "Closed but undone."

"So there was something you never felt was right," Mom said. She spoke quickly. Maybe she was aware that, at any moment, Tamara could cut off the conversation and kick us out. "There was something left undone?"

"The motel," Tom croaked.

"The Amistad," I said.

Tom nodded. "I should've gone…"

"Enough." Tamara stepped closer, putting herself between Mom and Tom. Mom was forced to straightened up and take a step back. Over her shoulder, to her husband, Tamara added, "You were sick, remember? You couldn't go."

"That's right. I couldn't." He shook his head. "But later…I should've reopened…" He broke into another coughing fit.

"Leave it be," Tamara demanded. Fierce. But also begging. Her eyes watery. "Leave it be." She turned toward us. "Tom got his first diagnosis when he was working that case. Remember?"

Mom nodded. "I remember. I was in shock. We all were. The doctors gave him 6 months to live. But he beat the cancer into remission."

Tom smiled. "Put off the inevitable…" He pushed at the armrests of his chair, straightening himself up. "But this…I can't put off…not any more…I need to…" He struggled to lift himself, only to slide back down. "…need to set things straight…"

"Stop!" Tamara grabbed my mom's arm and pulled her away. "For God's sake, Charlie. Leave him alone. Can't you see it's killing him?" Her voice was rising. "Go now. Leave him alone. Give him some peace. You're all the same—you, Ken Tora, everyone—totally disrespectful of my husband's condition."

Mom stared at Tamara. "Ken Tora? What was that about Ken Tora?"

Tamara let go of my mom. She drew her arms across her chest. "Nothing."

"Tammy. You'd better tell me before I lose my patience with you."

Tamara opened her mouth. Shut it. Then glanced at Mom's shiny badge pinned to her chest. Finally, she said, through clenched teeth, "He called and called, insisting. He just had to talk to Tom. I knew it would be bad for him. So I told him no." She shook her head. "No, no, no."

"What did Ken want to talk about?"

"Well, what do you think? I didn't ask. But I'm sure it was about that missing boy. He said it was important."

Next to me, Tom muttered, "Urgent and important..."

With Mom gone from Tom's side, it left an opening. I stepped into it, and crouching down, put a hand on the man's skeletal arm.

I said, "You said you should've gone to the hotel. But you didn't."

He nodded.

I pressed on. "But Mom said that your report included testimony from motel staff that they saw Herman."

"I'm ashamed to say...." He paused to catch his breath. "...I needed to close the case. Quick. I couldn't manage... so..." He sighed. "So I got the testimony."

"Got it?"

"Secondhand."

Tamara had gone quiet. She was staring at Tom, tears streaking her face. Mom's eyes had gone wide. She said, "But Tom, you could've put me on the case."

Tom raised a hand, as if to respond with a gesture. "We were..." He dropped his hand, exhausted. "...stretched thin. Remember all the break-ins and robberies? The money stolen from churches. Not enough cops to cover all the cases. And with me gone..."

"A secondhand testimony," I reminded him. "Who gave you the testimony?"

"The kid..." Tom coughed again. "The kid's friend... Herman's friend..."

I waited. My heart hammering in my chest. I didn't dare

speak the name. I didn't want to influence what Tom would say next. Needed to hear him say it. Say the name.

And then he did.

"Jack," Tom said, letting it out like a long exhalation.

Like a huge relief. Like a last breath.

18

In the cruiser heading back into town, Mom stared straight ahead. A white-knuckled grip on the wheel. The car bumped in and out of potholes. The trees whizzed past us.

"You OK?" I asked.

"I can't believe it." She shook her head. "And yet, I should've known."

"About Jack."

"No, about Tom. He was sick. He was in shock about his diagnosis. Looking back, I knew he was cutting corners, dropping balls, but we were all in shock." She glanced at me. "This is the thing about certain jobs, Park. If you're a cop or a nurse or a firefighter, you have bad days just like everyone else. But the difference is that you still have to give a 100 percent. And if you can't, things may go wrong. Horribly wrong."

I nodded. From what Mom had told me over the years, Tom had been an excellent chief of police. Diligent. Fair-minded. But during the darkest days of his working life, he'd taken a shortcut. One shortcut. And things had gone wrong.

Mom slowed at the end of the dirt road and turned onto the blacktop. She accelerated. The ride was smoother now.

"Jack took advantage of him," I said.

Mom nodded. "He trusted Jack. I can see how Tom would admire what Herman's friends did to track him down. The dedication. The determination. How many friends would go to such lengths to find a runaway?"

"That alone might've been a clue that something was suspicious."

"That's a cynical point of view." She glanced at me. Then looked back out the windshield at the road. "But I agree. We cops need to consider the cynical point of view, and Tom didn't. He was in a bad place and wanted to believe in humanity's goodness." She sighed. "If only Tammy hadn't kept Ken from talking to Tom..."

Mom's radio crackled and Deputy Douglas's voice came through.

"Chief, we got the forensics report."

It was a relief to hear Mom switch into her all-business chief-of-police voice. She said, "Go ahead, Deputy, give me the highlights."

"Blunt trauma to the back of the head. Likely with a hard, flat object."

Which made me think of what Groff had pulled out of the lake. I said, "Like a shovel?"

"Oh, hi, Parker," Deputy Douglas said through the radio. "Yeah, I guess. In fact..." Pause. Click, click, click. Deputy Douglas must be at his desk, clicking through documents. Finally, he said, "Here it is. I ran fingerprints on the Lakeview Inn's shed, Chief, like you suggested."

I glanced at Mom. She hadn't told me about this, but it

was smart. Someone had broken into the shed and stolen a shovel. Which Groff had fished out of the water. The thief's identity could be a clue to the murder.

"Yes," Mom said. "Any match?"

"We got a set of clear prints from the tool rack where the shovel was taken from. You won't believe this. The prints belong to—"

I said, "Ken Tora."

"Yeah," Deputy Douglas said, sounding disappointed that I stole his thunder. "Ken Tora."

He signed off.

Mom slowed the cruiser to a crawl. Then pulled the car to the shoulder of the road. She turned to me.

"So Ken stole the shovel and threw it in the lake? That makes no sense."

"But maybe this does: Ken stole the shovel, sent me an anonymous note, grabbed one of Lil's rowboats, and went to Gull Island."

"To do what?"

A chill ran down my neck as I realized what the answer was. An icy cold touched my bones. Goosebumps prickled my arms.

"To dig. Ken went to Gull Island to dig."

19

"If I'd only known," Mom said for the umpteenth time. "Then we wouldn't be here now."

"But we are here. And we may finally learn what happened."

Here was Gull Island. As soon as we got back to Allington, Mom had steered her cruiser down to the docks. Then a brief stop at Scottie's Ice Cream Shop. Which surprised me. But it turned out Scottie had a pair of shovels in his storage room. Of course he did. Scottie had all kinds of weird things lying around in his storage room, just in case he'd need them.

Then we jumped into the police department's speedboat and flew across the water to the island.

Now we were standing in the clearing by the cabin. Each armed with a shovel. Birds tweeted in the trees. The sun was high in the sky. Not noon yet, but getting there. A beautiful day.

But an ominous feeling darkened my mood.

We headed for where I'd found Ken's body. Crime-scene

tape still cordoned off the area. Mom ducked under it and then held the tape so I could follow.

Moving closer to where Ken was found, Mom crouched down, cocking her head as she studied the ground. The dirt and rotting leaves were disturbed where Ken had fallen. A root from a nearby tree snaked under the crime-scene tape, disappearing into the ground. Nothing else, though.

"The dirt is flat and hard," Mom said, tapping the surface with her shovel. "If anyone tried to dig here, it would be obvious."

I looked around the area. Using my shovel, I pushed aside the brambles nearby and looked at the dirt. Also intact.

We returned to the front of the cabin. Apart from bottles and cans and other trash, the clearing looked undisturbed, too. No sign of digging. Could we have made a mistake? Maybe Ken didn't come to the island to dig, after all.

Mom must've had the same thought, because she said, "Maybe he intended to dig but didn't get around to it?"

I shook my head. "But someone dumped the shovel in the lake. As if they wanted to hide the evidence."

I spun around myself, looking for ideas. Ken could've tried to dig anywhere on the island. But if that was the case, why did I find him lying behind the cabin?

The cabin.

I faced the ruined house. Beyond the doorless doorway, the inside was still dark. It was always dark in there.

"Park? What's on your mind?"

I ignored Mom. It was as if an idea was swimming to the surface, and I was afraid to disturb it. Couldn't let it get away.

I headed into the cabin.

In the shadowy interior, I looked around. Stairs to the right, rising to a trapdoor. Plywood-covered windows. An old stained mattress on the floor. Discarded cans and plastic bags.

I kicked a can aside. Ran the tip of my shoe along the dirt floor. Broken boards jutting out of the walls showed where the wood floor had once lain. The cabin had once been a home—or a fishing lodge. Now it was a ruin full of trash and dirt.

And a dirty old mattress.

I crouched down. The thing was so stained, it was more gray and brown than its original white. Even the white parts were so off-white as to be gray. I dreaded to touch it. But I knew I needed to.

I grasped the edge and heaved it aside. Light foam. It slid easily.

In the darkness, I couldn't see much underneath. But I touched the ground and felt the dirt—how loose it was.

"Mom?" I called out.

"Here."

I stiffened, almost jumped at her voice. She was right behind me. I hadn't heard her approach. And I wondered: Did Ken not hear the killer approach, either?

"The dirt is loose here," I said.

"Then let's get digging."

We set our smartphones on the ground and turned on their flashlights. Mom had a flashlight in her belt. She turned that on, too, and found a wooden beam to rest it on. The lights brightened the cabin. Now I could see it clearly: rutted dirt with furrows from a shovel blade. Someone had been digging up the floor.

Not just someone. Ken Tora.

I shoved my shovel into the ground and pulled up dirt.

Mom started digging, too. The mound of dirt grew between us. And grew. And grew.

I had to stop to wipe the sweat off my forehead.

Mom grunted as she heaved more dirt aside. The dug-up dirt on the surface gave way to harder dirt. As if Ken had dug down, but not far enough. Or he'd been interrupted before he could finish the job and then someone—the killer—had packed the dirt back into the hole. And laid the mattress over it.

I lifted my shovel and punched it into the ground—and hit something.

"Mom."

"I heard it."

She crouched down, and after putting on latex gloves, began pulling out dirt with her hands. "A plastic bag. Something inside. It's big. Help me clear this."

She gave me a pair of latex gloves. I put them on and crouched down, joining her effort to claw the dirt away from the object.

By the light of our flashlights, the object grew larger. And longer. Until it became clear what we'd found.

Mom scraped off dirt from the big plastic bag. An extra-large bag for yard waste. Things inside. Long dark things. Something rounded, too.

"Is that...?"

"A skull. And bones. Lots of bones."

Mom found an opening in the bag and dug a latex-covered hand inside, rooting around. She pulled out an object. A filthy wallet. But the plastic sleeve for the ID was still clean and clear.

The photo on the driver's license struck me like a punch to the gut.

"Herman," I said. "We found him."

20

"Herman's—" Judy's hands shook. She touched her throat. "—body? You found his—his—body? But he's in Mexico..."

Mom had gathered them—Judy, Trevor, Priscilla, and Jack—in the Lakeview Inn's lounge. She told them what we found on Gull Island. Now she was watching the old friends closely. So was I. Deputy Douglas stood by the door, in case one of them decided to bolt.

But none of them made a move. Judy's bangles jingled and jangled as she fussed with her scarf. Priscilla looked down at her lap, her shoulders hunched, as if a great weight pressed down on her. Trevor stared straight ahead, a deer caught in headlights.

They all looked shocked.

Except Jack. He simply frowned and muttered, "I can't believe it."

"What about you, Trevor?" Mom asked.

"I'm—I'm—" he stuttered, unable to get the words out. His eyes flickered. A glance over at where Jack was sitting on the love seat. Then he said, "Herman's body? He's dead?"

Priscilla gripped Jack's arm. She said, "I can't believe it. He's dead? He's really dead?"

I frowned. People in shock might say and do strange things. But would they use such similar words? It was almost as if they were falling back on a script.

Still, Judy was trembling. Trevor stared wide-eyed at his shoes. And Priscilla cowered at Jack's side. Genuine shock—or something else. Fear?

Only Jack kept his cool.

"We know he left town," he said. "So then, how can his body turn up in Allington?"

"Do we know for certain that he left town?" Mom asked.

Jack shrugged. "I followed him to the Mexican border, didn't I?"

"Did you? The police report from back then states that Herman's presence was confirmed by staff. But staff testimony was provided secondhand—by you."

"Sure," he said. "I reported what I was told. Herman stayed at the Amistad. Then moved on. If his body was buried out on Gull Island, then he must've come back home. He must've been roughing it, sleeping in the woods and out on the island. Maybe a crazy drifter killed him."

"A crazy drifter?"

"Read the news. It's full of crazy homeless people killing hikers and campers."

"What newspapers do you read?" I asked.

Mom gave me a look, a warning. Don't let it get personal.

Then she said, "We're reopening the disappearance of Herman Hertz. It's now a murder case. And I want you all to stay in Allington and make yourselves available for questioning."

Priscilla gasped. "You don't think we—?"

"We were best friends," Trevor mumbled. "We'd never deliberately harm…"

"We were a study group," Jack cut in. "I was the economics and history whiz. Priscilla was all about languages. Judy's specialty was English literature. Trevor was biology and chemistry. And Herman was all about math and computer science. We helped each other get through middle school and high school courses and exams. That's hardly a motive for murder."

"Who said anything about a motive for murder?" Mom asked.

Jack smiled. It was a cold smile. "I did. I'm not a fool, Chief Lee. I know how this looks, and all I can tell you is that we all—me, Priscilla, Judy, Trevor, and Ken—did what we could to find Herman when he ran away." He ran a hand over his slicked-back hair. "You should be more worried about our safety. Ken is dead. Now it turns out Herman died, too. Someone's obviously out to get us." He looked at his friends, one by one: Priscilla, Trevor, then Judy. "If we're not careful, the killer will get us, too."

"You mentioned motive," I said. "What motive would someone have to kill you?"

"Revenge," Jack said.

"Revenge? For what?"

"You'd better ask Gordon Groff about that."

21

Dark clouds blanketed the sky over Allington. The late afternoon light was failing sooner than usual, the shadows of an early dusk settling over the Lakeview Inn. A damp breeze blew across the back porch, and I zipped up my jacket. Aunt Lil and I stood by the back railing, eyeing the activity on Gull Island.

The Allington PD speedboat was moored by the island. So was a state police boat. Bright lights glared among the trees. Forensics at work. Occasionally, a person in uniform appeared at the water's edge. Then vanished again.

Aunt Lil said, "Poor kid. He didn't get far."

"I'm not sure he intended to run away."

"You mean it was a story to cover up his disappearance? If that's the case, then Jack looks awfully guilty."

I nodded. "But what he said about Groff…"

Mom had questioned the group about their relationship with Groff, and they fleshed out the old story I'd read about in *The Gazette*'s archives: Groff, the high school teacher, hated the kids in the study group. He seemed unnaturally interested in the girls. He was caught snooping around Judy's bedroom, and it ruined his teaching career.

None of them—Jack, Priscilla, Trevor, or even Judy—could explain why Groff had taken such an interest in them. Though Jack suggested the resentment had something to do with their backgrounds. All five kids in the Circle came from the working class side of Allington, and their academic success rubbed Groff the wrong way. Priscilla wasn't so sure. She said he was simply "a perv" who took a "creepy interest" in the girls.

Now I told Aunt Lil, "Groff's been hanging around the inn a lot lately. If he wanted to go fishing, why do it on your dock? Why not go somewhere quiet—where he might actually catch a fish?"

"Instead of a shovel?" Aunt Lil said.

"Yeah, that's something I've wondered about, too. Was he in the right place at the right time to haul up that shovel? Or did he put the shovel there in the first place?"

"To do what? Point the finger at Ken's friends?"

I shrugged. "I don't know. But I do know this: Groff is somehow involved in all this. We've heard Jack's version of the story. I'd like to hear Groff's."

Groff might reveal something new or even the key to the whole mystery—which would be a real scoop for *The Gazette*. Plus, Herman's body being unearthed would put pressure on the killer. Assuming it was the same person who murdered Ken—and it was because Ken discovered where Herman was buried—the killer might become desperate. Talking to Groff couldn't wait.

I said, "He lives out in the woods, doesn't he? I remember driving past his driveway."

Aunt Lil stared at me, her eyebrows pressed into a frown. "Parker, the planetary alignment...well, you know, Groff's a

Scorpio...all I'm saying is, you'd better wait for your mom to come back from Gull Island. Or you can get Deputy Douglas's help."

"Mom will be busy all night. And Douglas is down at the station, dealing with Jack and his friends. I can't wait."

Aunt Lil checked the time on her wristwatch. "I've got guests arriving in half an hour. Can you at least wait a couple of hours? Then I'll come with you."

I put a hand on her arm. "It's fine, Aunt Lil. I'm just dropping by Groff's house to talk. That's all. A friendly chat. What could possibly go wrong?"

She winced. "I hate it when you say that."

22

The rutted road through the woods grew full of massive potholes. My Dad's car bumped and shuddered, and at one point dipped into a hole and a rock scraped the bottom. A teeth-gritting sound. Like the ripping of metal.

Dad's car was an old Subaru from God knew when. It didn't need any more scratches or dents, that was for sure.

I pulled over to the side of the road and got out. Up ahead in the distance, I could make out a cabin in the woods. Groff's home. Not far on foot. I slammed my door shut, and the sound reverberated among the trees. A crow, startled, cawed and flew up.

Apart from the crow, I saw no one.

No one for miles.

Groff lived alone in a remote part of the woods. The guy must enjoy his solitude.

I trudged down the road. A well-trodden path appeared among the trees and I followed it, navigating roots and rocks. The cabin grew closer. The path cut across a ridge and then switchbacked down to the cabin. A sign on a stake jammed into the dirt by the path said:

PRIVATE PROPERTY: STAY OUT!

I kept going. It was getting darker. The charcoal clouds in the sky and the thick canopy of trees crowded out the light. Dusk became deeper the closer I got to the cabin. It was cool and damp. As if I'd stepped into a gully.

Looking up, I realized that was about right: the cabin was flanked by ridges. Not the best place for a home.

Unless you wanted to hide.

The shutters on the windows were open, but the curtains were drawn. No movement within. So I walked up to the door and knocked. I listened for footsteps. No sound from within. Just a heavy dripping somewhere off to my left. I knocked again and waited. Nothing.

A path of smooth stones led me around the cabin. A barrel stood under the eaves, catching rainwater. Plop, plop, plop. Presumably the dripping I'd heard. Another window. This one shuttered. I continued along the stone path to the next corner and turned it.

A porch ran along this side. The railing had split in some places, splinters hanging loose, the wood rotting. An ancient rocking chair sat on the porch.

The view from the porch was of dense forest. Trees everywhere. Moss-covered rocks. I looked around. No signs of life.

I ducked under the railing and stepped onto the porch. The boards creaked ominously.

The screen door groaned. I knocked. No answer. I knocked again and waited. Still no answer. I tried the back door's handle, but it didn't budge. Locked.

Bad luck. Groff must be off somewhere on a job. But maybe there was a window on the other side I could open. It wouldn't hurt to peek inside.

Thinking I'd backtrack, I turned around. And froze.

In the shadows between trees stood a figure. Gordon Groff. Hunched shoulders. A grim look on his face. In his hands, he held an axe. He trudged toward me.

"Can't you read?" he growled. "The sign says *stay out*."

"I came to talk," I said, swallowing the last of my saliva. My mouth had suddenly gone dry. "That's all."

"I know you and your dad and that newspaper. I don't have anything to say to you. You can take your *Gazette* newspaper and shove it."

He was advancing faster now. The axe still gripped in his hands. Knuckles turning white.

"Did you hear about Herman?" I said.

That stopped him in his tracks. His frown grew deeper. "What about him?"

"We found his body."

His jaw dropped. For an instant. Then he closed his mouth.

He said, "Oh, yeah? Where?"

"Out on Gull Island."

Slowly, he nodded. "Good."

I wasn't sure if he meant it was good that Herman was found—or good that he'd been buried on the island.

"You've said what there is to say." He hefted his axe and pointed it toward me. "Now leave me be."

"I want to talk to you about Ken, and Jack, and the others."

"Get out," he hissed, taking a step toward me. He was only a few paces from the porch now.

I tried to swallow again. But it was like trying to drink sand. My mouth was too dry.

"What happened back then—with you and those kids? I want your side of the story."

"Get out," he roared. "Get out before I—"

He stepped toward me, rage contorting his face. He raised his axe.

"Before you what?" a voice said.

Groff whipped around.

Mom stood among the trees. Her right hand casually resting on her gun holster. Next to her stood Aunt Lil.

"Are you gonna use that axe, Gordon," Mom said, "or are you gonna listen to reason?"

Groff stared at her. Glanced back at me.

He lifted the axe and let out a roar—like a wounded animal—and threw it aside. It hit the ground with a thunk.

Hands clenched into fists by his side, he glared at my mom.

"Well?" he demanded. "What now?"

Mom smiled. "Now we talk."

23

Groff didn't invite us inside his cabin—he said he knew his Constitutional Rights—but he opened the back door so he could put away his axe. I peeked over his shoulder and saw a small, clean kitchen and neat living room with shelves stuffed with books. On a coffee table lay a brick-sized biography of George Washington. Which made sense. Groff was a former history teacher. No doubt he still enjoyed reading history.

He emerged onto the porch again. He let the screen door smack shut—cutting off my view of the inside—and then leaned against the doorframe. Arms crossed.

He said, "All right. Talk."

Aunt Lil and I stood near the steps to the porch, a good distance between us and Groff. But Mom placed herself closer to the man, apparently unafraid.

She said, "Parker came to ask you about Ken Tora and his friends. I'd like to hear what you have to say."

"You know the story."

"I know the old reports. I know what was printed in *The Gazette*."

Groff spat on the porch boards. "That's what I think of *The Gazette*."

Mom nodded. "If *The Gazette* got your story wrong, why don't you tell us the truth?"

"Like you care. I know how Allington works: Mr. Lee runs the paper and Mrs. Lee runs law and order. Your kids handle the rest. An average guy like me doesn't stand a chance."

"An average guy who breaks into a teenage girl's bedroom?"

"Now, look here—that wasn't what really happened."

"Oh?" Mom said. "So you didn't break into Judy Budgie's bedroom?"

"I did—but..." He shook his head. "What's the point? You won't believe me, anyway. Those kids had the whole town wrapped around their fingers."

I stepped up next to Mom and said, "People saw Jack as a hero because he traveled so far to find his friend, Herman."

Groff frowned. "I'm talking about before that. When Herman was part of it. When they were all part of it."

"Part of what?" I asked. "Their study group?"

He snorted. "The Circle, a study group? Don't make me laugh."

"So they weren't a study group?"

"Of course they were." He scratched his chin. "They were, and they weren't. See, they did study together, and probably started off helping each other with their homework. Back in elementary school, they were the freaks and geeks. Working class, but too bookish and nerdy to be popular. Guess they banded together out of necessity. By middle school, they were meeting regularly. A tight little circle. But with Ken and Jack taking the lead. Priscilla seemed like the glue that held them together. Herman and Trevor and Judy

—they were the followers. I'd see them in the cafeteria or in the hallways or outside in recess, and they'd be huddled together."

"Sounds harmless," Lil said.

"Well, you'd think so, wouldn't you?" Groff shot back at her, as if he expected nothing less from her. "But see, I had my eyes and ears open. I started noticing something. Similarities in their homework. First, I thought they were just studying together. Sharing notes. Nothing wrong about that. But their essays started to sound more and more similar. I suspected one of them was writing the history stuff. Probably Jack. He was the sharpest of them when it came to history."

"You're talking about plagiarism," Mom said.

Groff nodded. "Plagiarism. And then worse."

"Worse?"

"They did well on quizzes. But not always perfect. It was the final exam that made me suspicious." He stared at us as if he wanted to make sure we were listening. Then said, "Perfect scores. All of them. Even that dunce, Trevor."

"They were cheating," I said.

"Right. But the final exam wasn't something I wrote. It was a state exam."

"You're saying they somehow got hold of the answers ahead of time?"

Groff shook his head. "The essay section would still vary. Judy's practice exam, for example. Her essay was awful. But she got a top score on the final. Along with the other kids. Which means they must've found a way to mess with the exam records."

"How could they do that?"

"I don't know. But I've got an idea. I think they hacked into the school computer system. Or the state system.

Herman could do it. He was a computer whiz. I went looking for evidence, but Herman wasn't easy to get close to. He caught me trying to look at his computer once, and that spooked him. He got wary of me. So I tried someone else. Judy was sloppy and scatter-brained. I thought maybe she would have something lying around."

"That's why you broke into her home?"

Groff nodded, eager now. "I'm telling the truth."

He looked from me, and then to Aunt Lil, and finally to Mom. His anger transformed into something else: desperation.

"You've got to believe me. I told the old chief of police back in the day—Tom Truby—but there was no evidence to back me up. He didn't believe me. I told him about other things, too."

"What other things?" Mom asked.

"Money disappearing. These kids came from homes where they didn't have a lot of money. But somehow they always had the money they needed to join clubs or trips to the capital. Later, a couple of them got partial scholarships to college, but even so, how could any of them afford their Ivy League tuition? Somehow, money was never an issue."

"You think they stole the money?"

"Remember the time several churches got hacked and their bank accounts were emptied?"

Mom nodded. Of course, she remembered. We all did. It had been a huge scandal—a horrible reminder of how vulnerable we all were to hackers. Amy's church had been hit hard.

Groff said, "I was sure Herman and his friends did that."

"But you have no evidence of it."

"No." Groff sighed and shook his head. "No evidence."

24

With Mom back on Gull Island, and Dad working later at *The Gazette*, I ate dinner at the Lakeview Inn. Aunt Lil's chef served breaded fish with a homemade tartar sauce, a green salad, and roasted potatoes with fresh rosemary. Delicious.

Aunt Lil and I sat in the dining room at the long table, sharing it with a few guests: a grandmother, her son, and her granddaughter traveling across country; a middle-aged couple on a modest honeymoon; and a two Anglican priests from England on their way to an interfaith conference. Outside, thunder cracked open the dark clouds and rain tapped against the window.

Amid the chatter of the guests, Aunt Lil and I leaned across the table toward each other to keep our heads close and our voices low.

Aunt Lil asked, "Do you believe Groff's story? He's been living in that cabin in the woods for years. The incident with the kids killed his career. Maybe he's gone a little crazy. I mean, his aura—did you see his aura?"

"I don't know. He seemed genuinely eager for us to

believe. I think he himself believes it. But he can't prove any of it." I dipped a forkful of fish in the tartar sauce, which had a nice, lemony tang to it. "His story does match what Jack said, though. In terms of Jack being the history buff and Herman being a computer whiz."

"But there's a long way from teenage computer whiz to becoming a hacker that breaks into the state's education system and manipulates exam results." Aunt Lil speared a small roasted potato with her fork. "Even I know that."

"True. It shouldn't be hard to find out just how good Herman was. And if he was capable of hacking—"

Footsteps pounding down the hallway. Judy appeared in the doorway, her hair in disarray, a look of distress on her face.

"Someone—" she panted. "—someone broke into my room."

The other guests stopped talking and looked up.

Aunt Lil calmly got to her feet, folded her napkin, and placed it next to her plate. Her bangles jangled and her muumuu billowed as she swept over to Judy. She smiled as she took Judy's arm. "That's awful. Let's go take a look and see what we can do."

She escorted Judy out of the room. It took only a couple of seconds, and throughout, Aunt Lil's focus was on Judy, showing empathy and concern. But I'm sure Aunt Lil was also thinking about the effect on the other guests. She might seem like a new-age kook, but Aunt Lil was savvy about her hotel business. In fact, she was savvy about a lot of things.

One of the Anglicans got up, muttering, "Left my laptop on the bed..." But the others seemed less concerned, and after the priest left, the conversations resumed.

I took another bite of my food. Then folded my napkin, too, and went looking for Aunt Lil.

Down the corridor from the dining room, the door to the lounge was open. I heard voices and stopped.

"She's checking my room," Judy said.

"Then why're you here?" Trevor's voice. He sounded anxious. Speaking in fast, breathless bursts. "She could be snooping."

"I've got nothing to hide."

Trevor made a little sound, a squeaky moan, like a puppy that's injured.

"I mean, I'm not hiding anything in my room, am I?" Judy said. She sounded uncertain. "You think there's a risk...?"

"I wouldn't be here," Trevor said. "I would be up there."

"You're right. I'll go." Pause. "Tell the others—" Pause again. "Tell them I'm tired and I'm staying in my room. Don't mention the break-in. OK?"

"OK."

I stepped back from the doorway just as Judy shot out of the lounge and strode toward the reception and the staircase to the upper floors. She didn't even see me.

I casually sauntered into the lounge.

"Oh, hi, Trevor."

He was sitting in an armchair. Dark shadows around his eyes. Gaunt, hollowed-out cheeks. His eye sockets seemed to be swallowing his entire face. He must be sleeping poorly.

"Hi," he said, sounding miserable.

"Where are your friends?"

One eyelid fluttered a little. A nervous tick.

"My friends? They're around."

"We're right here," Jack said, walking into the room. Priscilla came behind him. She said, "Where's Judy?"

Trevor looked miserable. "She's in her room. She's tired."

"Well, go get her," Jack said. "We're going for dinner and drinks at the Breeze."

"She said she wanted to rest."

Priscilla went to Trevor, crouching down to be closer. She put a hand on his knee and said, "Buddy, we don't want to leave Judy out. You know how anxious she gets about being left out. What's more important than including everyone? We're a family, right?"

Trevor nodded. "Right."

Priscilla smiled. "So, go ahead and fetch her. We'll borrow some umbrellas and walk over to the bar together."

Trevor got to his feet. He crossed the room. Head ducked down, as if he hoped no one would look at him. Then he vanished through the doorway.

Priscilla smiled at me.

"Poor guy. Ken's death has torn him apart. All the questions from the police aren't making it any less traumatic." She turned to Jack. "Isn't that right, Jack?"

Jack had sat down and was flipping through a magazine, looking bored. He nodded. "Totally. Poor guy."

Priscilla's eyebrows wrinkled into a little frown.

"All we want to do is help the police catch whoever did this," she said, eyes still on Jack.

"I was wondering about something," I said.

Priscilla turned her attention back to me. Eyebrows raised.

"About Herman," I said. I made sure to sound as casual as I could. "Finding his body has raised a lot of questions. I'm sure you're tired of hearing them, but if answering them can help find the killer..."

"Of course," Priscilla said.

I plowed on. "I hear he was a computer whiz. And he had a big interest in hacking."

Priscilla blinked. "Sure. He loved computers. But what does that have to do with his death?"

I shrugged. "Just something I heard. About him being a master hacker."

I glanced over and saw Jack had stopped reading his magazine. He was staring at me, a frown on his face. Then he ducked his head and kept reading. An attempt to look disinterested. But he'd definitely reacted to my comment about Herman being a hacker.

Then Trevor returned with Judy, and Priscilla herded her friends out of the lounge, excusing herself to me. "If we're going to have time for dinner and drinks at the Breeze, we need to leave now."

I was left alone in the lounge.

25

"What can I get you?" Ray asked from behind the bar.

I put a finger to my lips, and he gave me a confused look, glancing at Aunt Lil and then back at me. I gestured for him to lean closer.

"We're keeping an eye on them," I whispered, pointing a thumb over my shoulder.

He followed my finger and saw. "Oh, Ken Tora's friends."

They were sitting in a booth—Jack and Priscilla on one side of the table, Judy and Trevor on the other—with drinks all around. A server brought out salads for Priscilla and Judy and burgers for Jack and Trevor, and the friends got busy eating.

"Anything new in the investigation?" Ray asked after he took our orders for drinks.

"Someone broke into Judy's room at the inn," I said. "Or at least, so she claims."

"No sign of a break-in," Aunt Lil added. "But why would she lie about such a thing?"

"I don't know. But she was reluctant to tell Jack and Priscilla."

I explained the conversation between Judy and Trevor I'd overheard outside the lounge.

"So much for the Circle being a tight-knit group," Aunt Lil said. "And here I was thinking an annual reunion made them exemplary friends. An example of conflicting star signs actually working together."

I cocked my head, looking at my aunt. "Aunt Lil, how do you know what all their star signs are?"

"My registration," she said. "My computer tracks it, so I know what kind of balance of Zodiacs I have at my inn."

Ray served me a pint of his lager. Aunt Lil got a small glass of port. He said, "Sometimes people stick together because it's easier. Sometimes they stick together because they're afraid to say goodbye."

"Or afraid of something else," I said.

I wasn't even sure what I meant. Just a gut feeling that there was fear at work. Fear of each other. But was there also fear of what happened to Ken? And to Herman? I glanced back at the group.

Jack was dipping a French fry in ketchup and saying something, his usual cocky smile in place. Priscilla, a patient smile on her face, seemed to be listening. Judy cowered in a corner, pecking at her salad. Trevor chugged a beer, nearly draining the bottle.

I didn't like Jack. He made me suspicious. But what if he was right—what if the members of the Circle were somehow at risk? Could a killer be trying to murder each of them, one by one? Jack had said it was about revenge...

"I wish I could be a fly on the wall and listen to what they're saying," I said, turning back to Ray and Aunt Lil.

"No problem," Ray said. "I'll be your fly."

He moved down the bar and lifted the flip-up section of the counter and crossed the floorboards, heading for the booth. But he didn't go straight to them. He stopped at the booth next to theirs and talked to a customer there. Then he sidled over to the next booth, and after a moment, Jack, Priscilla, Judy, and Trevor all looked up.

At this distance, and with music playing and people talking, I couldn't hear a word of what Ray was saying. He was nodding. Then turned around and came back.

Once he was behind the bar counter again, he said, "Another round of drinks. Except Jack. He's had one beer and doesn't want more. Wants to keep a sharp mind. Priscilla ordered strong cocktails for her and Judy—Long Island Ice Teas—and Trevor wanted another beer. But sorry, I didn't overhear them say anything interesting. Just stuff about when Mom might allow them to leave Allington."

I nodded. "I'm surprised none of them has tried to leave town yet."

"That would look pretty suspicious," Aunt Lil said.

"True. The first person to bolt is basically inviting Mom to arrest them. Ray, did you notice anything else?"

Ray was busy preparing the drinks for the table. He shook his head as he mixed the cocktails. Then said, "I stopped at the booth next to theirs and pretended to chat with Shirley, but meanwhile, I was listening. I didn't hear anything interesting, though."

"Shirley?" I said. "You mean Shirley Hertz?"

"Sure. She's sitting in a booth by herself."

I turned around on my barstool. So did Lil. Across the Breeze, I caught sight of Shirley. She was leaning out of her booth, reaching around the seat to where Trevor was sitting.

Her hand was in the pocket of his jacket. In a flash, she'd pulled back her hand. She clenched an object in her fist, then shoved it into her purse.

But I was pretty sure I knew what it was. So did Aunt Lil.

"Trevor's key," she mumbled. "She stole it."

26

Up ahead in the darkness, the shadowy figure slipped under a lamppost, lighting her up. Shirley in a dark raincoat. Then she merged with the rain and the night.

My shoes thumped the wooden dock as I jogged after Shirley. I didn't want Shirley to hear us. But Aunt Lil's bangles and necklaces, as she hurried after me, clutching her bag to her chest, sounded like a hundred wind chimes.

Fortunately, the bad weather covered us. The rain and wind lashed us. A man hurried past us, his jacket pulled over his head for cover as he headed in the direction we'd come from. Probably heading for a drink at the Breeze.

At the end of the town docks, I tugged Aunt Lil's sleeve and pointed.

A shadow flitted across the road and then down the sidewalk, heading across the bridge that spanned the river emptying into Lake Allington. On the other side, the road swept past the hulking house at the water's edge: the Lakeview Inn.

A car sailed past us, its tires shushing on the watery

road. Its red brake lights flashed once before going over the bridge. Then it sped up and drove into the dark.

Aunt Lil and I followed Shirley at a distance, but when she swept up the front steps to the inn and vanished inside, we both broke into a run. Splashing through puddles.

We pounded up the steps. I yanked open the front door, and Aunt Lil and I stumbled inside.

We stood there, dripping.

The reception was warm and dry. And also quiet. No one in sight.

Aunt Lil shook herself, like a dog, her hair and jewelry and billowy dress spraying water. I ran a hand over my face. Then mopped my eyes with my sleeve.

"Upstairs?" I asked.

"Upstairs," Aunt Lil confirmed.

We climbed the stairs. But slower now. Careful not to alert Shirley.

"Trevor's room?" I whispered.

"Second floor."

We came to the first-floor landing. I peered down the corridors—carpeted floors, Victorian wainscoting—and caught one of the Anglican priests coming out of her room. When she saw me, she smiled.

"Not here," I said.

Aunt Lil and I hurried upward, taking the stairs two at a time. All the while, my mind was racing. So someone did break into Judy's room. Shirley. And now she was going after Trevor.

Why?

I thought of Herman's body and Ken's, and then pictured Shirley out on Gull Island. Standing behind Ken. Raising a shovel and bringing it down on his head.

Revenge? Because she believed Ken and his friends

killed her boyfriend all those years ago? Or could it be an entirely different motive? Did she stop Ken from unearthing Herman because it would reveal the truth?

Herman and Manfred. Two brothers. And one girl. Shirley. That was one of the oldest motives in human history: jealousy. But then, wouldn't it make more sense that Manfred was the one responsible for murdering his brother, and murdering Ken, and breaking into Judy's room?

"Doesn't make sense," I muttered to myself.

At the second-floor landing, we turned down a corridor. Just in time to see someone slip through a door.

"That's Trevor's room," Aunt Lil whispered.

We approached the door. My heart was pounding. The palms of my hands tingled.

Aunt Lil brought out a crystal from her bag and waved it across the door. Apparently that would help us somehow. Then she put a hand on the door handle and looked at me, waiting for my signal to go inside.

I bit my lip. Were we walking into a room to face a killer? We had nothing to prove Shirley's connection to Ken's death. If we barged in now, would we ruin any chances we had of discovering her purpose?

I grabbed Aunt Lil's arm.

"Wait."

27

One of the rooms down the corridor was unoccupied, and Aunt Lil and I stood just inside the door, peeking out. Waiting for Shirley to reappear.

"What if she leaves the inn?" Aunt Lil whispered.

"Then we catch up and confront her," I said. "But at least we'll have a better chance of seeing what she's been doing in Trevor's room."

"You think she's stealing something?"

I shrugged. "Or planting something. But I have no idea."

Aunt Lil pulled me back. Trevor's door was opening. My stomach tensed as Shirley stepped out and closed the door behind her, locking it again. In the hallway, she stopped. Hesitated. She looked to the left and then the right. Flexed her fingers. Shifted from foot to foot. A frown on her face.

"What's she doing?" Lil asked.

"Looks like she's trying to make up her mind about something..."

Shirley stopped moving. She clenched her fists. Apparently made up her mind. She moved swiftly down the corridor toward us.

Aunt Lil and I ducked back, and Aunt Lil carefully closed the door. I held my breath, listening for the sound of footsteps. The carpeting was soft. There wasn't much to hear. But there it was: the whisper of feet passing our room.

I counted three beats, then nudged Aunt Lil.

She opened the door a crack.

Down the corridor, Shirley stood over a door. She was fiddling with the lock.

"Trying to pick the lock," I said.

"That's Jack's room," Aunt Lil said. "And she's not picking the lock."

Shirley pulled open the door. Too fast for lock picking. She must've lifted Jack's key, too.

She vanished inside the room.

"Let's see what she's doing," I whispered.

But before I could leave the room, someone rushed past our door. A man striding down the corridor. Aunt Lil grabbed my arm and squeezed. I nodded. Even from the back, I knew him at once. No mistaking that slicked-back hair.

Jack.

If our door had stood open more than a narrow crack, he would've seen us. But he didn't stop to look. He headed straight for his room. And Shirley.

He pulled open the door and slipped inside. The door clicked shut.

"I've got a bad feeling about this," I said.

"Me, too," Aunt Lil said, clasping one of her talisman necklaces in her hand.

I stepped out into the corridor. Listened. All was quiet. I dug out my phone from my pocket and sent Mom a quick text message. I didn't dare call, in case my voice would be heard. But Mom texted right back:

> I'm on my way. Stay where you are. Don't get involved.

Then something crashed to the floor somewhere, and a woman screamed.

"Shirley," I said, shoving my phone into my pocket.

I broke into a run. Aunt Lil, judging by jangling, was right behind me, the two of us dashing down the corridor. I yanked open the door to Jack's room, and we both strode inside.

Disarray. A suitcase open on the bed. Clothes pulled out. The lamp from the desk was lying on the floor, smashed. A pair of legs visible behind the bed flailed and kicked.

Jack's slicked-back hair bobbed up. Then he leaned in again, pressing down.

I moved forward.

Jack had pinned Shirley to the ground. He was hissing something at her. And he had his hands around her throat, squeezing as she flailed, trying to beat him off.

"Jack," I yelled. "Stop!"

But he didn't stop.

Aunt Lil grabbed his shoulders and heaved him off. He staggered back and then swung a fist at her.

She stepped back just in time. His arm arced past her. Hitting air.

But her foot caught the cord of the lamp, and she tripped.

Jack took advantage and leaped forward. He grabbed the front of her dress to hold her and drew back an arm to punch.

I scooped up the half-broken lamp and slammed it

against his head. The remaining glass shattered. The metal and hard plastic socket rammed into his skull, and he staggered sideways, losing his grip on my aunt.

Aunt Lil grabbed his right arm and swung him around, twisting his hand up his back. Then hammered him against the wall.

He let out a grunt.

"Don't move," she said, and I realized that somehow, at some point, Mom must've shown her sister a trick or two.

"Let me go," Jack demanded, his voice muffled against the wall. "I was acting in self-defense. She broke into my room. Let me go."

I went around the bed and crouched down by Shirley. She was rubbing her neck, breathing in quick, ragged breaths.

"You OK?"

She nodded. I helped her off the floor and into a chair, making her comfortable while we waited for Mom to arrive.

28

Deputy Douglas led Jack out in handcuffs.

Jack struggled. "I want a lawyer," he growled.

Shirley sat on the bed. I sat next to her. Aunt Lil had gone to check on the other guests, since the commotion had brought several people out of their rooms.

Mom crossed her arms and frowned down at Shirley.

"You'd better explain yourself."

"I know," Shirley murmured, gazing down at her lap. "I know this looks bad…"

"Tell me where you were the morning Ken Tora died."

Shirley looked up, her eyes wide. "Ken? I didn't kill Ken, if that's what you're thinking."

"Just answer my question."

"I was at home with Manfred. It was a regular day. We got up around 7 am, had breakfast, and then went to the stationery store to get ready for business that day."

"Can anyone confirm that?"

"Manfred. Also, our neighbor. We said hello when I went out to get the morning paper. But you've got to believe me—" She turned to me, a pleading look in her eyes. "—I didn't kill Ken."

Mom stared at her. Then motioned for me to follow her, and I got up.

We went into the bathroom. It was a small space. Jack's toiletries stood on a shelf: a razor, a can of shaving foam, a face moisturizer, a toothbrush, and a bottle of sleeping pills.

"What do you think?" Mom whispered.

"She's telling the truth."

"Instinct or fact?"

"Instinct. But nothing concrete ties her to the murder on Gull Island, anyway."

Mom nodded. "Agreed."

Mom left the bathroom first. I glanced over my shoulder, noticing that bottle of sleeping pills again. Now, why did that attract my attention again? I shook my head. The whole situation had muddled my brain. I'd better follow Mom and focus on what Shirley had to say.

Coming back into the room, Mom said, "We don't believe you killed anyone, Shirley. But you've been breaking into people's rooms. It's time to come clean."

Shirley let out a breath, and her shoulders dropped.

"Thank goodness," she said. "I'm new to this kind of thing..."

"What exactly were you doing?" I asked, sitting down next to her again.

"I was looking for something." She shrugged. "Evidence, I guess. Anything that could explain what happened to Herman."

Saying his name, her voice snagged on something. She put a hand to her mouth.

"Herman," she said again, slowly shaking her head. Her voice wavered. On the verge of breaking. "I can't believe that all this time he was right here in Allington...right here with me..." Her eyes filled with tears.

She wiped them away and then straightened up.

"I knew one of members of the Circle did it," she said, her voice firm. "I never trusted Jack—or any of them, for that matter—and I told Herman to be careful."

"Be careful?" I said. "Why?"

Shirley looked away, suddenly evasive. "Well..."

"Shirley, why did Herman need to be careful?"

Mom added, "We need to know the truth. The full truth. Or we can't catch whoever killed Herman and Ken."

Shirley met Mom's gaze. "You think the same person..."

"I don't know. But it seems likely."

Shirley took a deep breath. Then she said, "Herman loved computers. Honestly, he was a genius. When other kids were playing games in elementary school, he was programming his own applications. By middle school, he'd mastered coding and even knew how to build his own hardware. There was nothing he couldn't do."

"You mean like hacking?" I asked.

Shirley bit her lip. She didn't say anything.

Mom said, "Tell us about the Circle and his hacking."

She nodded. "At first, they were just a study group. No name or anything. He helped his friends with math homework and anything computer related, and they helped him with the subjects he struggled with. But he was impatient. They all were. When we started dating in high school, he was already hacking into systems to change grades and exam results."

"He told you about it?"

"Yeah, once. I noticed his grades shooting through the roof. He hardly ever did any homework, especially not in the subjects he didn't care about. I had to work so hard for mediocre grades." She sighed. "Herman offered to help me. He said he could make my grades better, and I knew he was talking about cheating. I said absolutely not. No way. I was raised to believe that hard work was the only way. Herman thought that was ridiculous. Funny—" She shook her head, a slight smile at the corner of her mouth. "Manfred, who's a hard worker like me, he turned out to be the right one for me." Then she grew serious again. "Herman never offered again. And I didn't tell anyone, even after he disappeared. Because some small part of me still believed he might come home, and then I didn't want him to get into trouble..."

"You said you told Herman to be careful," I prompted her.

"I told him to be careful. I remember what he said: 'Don't worry. I'm careful. I erase my tracks, and those amateurs handling security are easy to hoodwink.' But he'd misunderstood. He thought I meant the cheating was risky. But I meant he should watch out for his so-called friends. I didn't trust them. I thought they were taking advantage of him. So I clarified what I meant."

"How did he react?"

"Not well. He got angry. He said they were a circle. They took an oath to remain 'unbroken.' Honestly, it sounded a little cultish to me. But then, after some time, something changed. Herman began to resent how the others treated him. And I think they all got a little paranoid as they got closer to the end of high school. It might be easy to maintain an unbroken circle in high school, but they'd be going off to college across the country. How could they keep tabs on each other then? I think Herman wanted out of the Circle, and I think one of the others found out."

"You suspect one of them killed Herman?"

Shirley nodded.

Mom frowned. "Why didn't you tell us all this before?"

Shirley ran her hands up and down her thighs, rubbing them. She looked down at her feet. "Like I said, I was protecting Herman. Plus, it took me a while to piece things together. I'm embarrassed to say that I believed Jack when he said he'd gone looking for Herman. I thought Herman had run away."

"Run away from the Circle?" I asked.

She shrugged. "From all of us."

"But Ken's death changed your mind?"

She nodded. "I began to wonder if there was more to Herman's disappearance. Of course, I'd wondered over the years. Suspected. But when Ken was murdered, I knew someone was hiding something. So I started to look around..."

She gestured vaguely at the suitcase that lay open on the bed behind us. I glanced over. And then, looking back at her, glanced back again. Something was sticking out from under a neatly folded shirt.

"Mom..."

Mom came over. Under her breath, she muttered, "Well, will you look at this..."

She pulled out a pair of latex gloves and snapped them on. Carefully, she eased the object out from under Jack's shirt. It was a notebook.

"Identical to the one we found in Ken's room," Mom said as she flipped it open. "Except this one's been used."

"It's the one he wrote in?"

"Seems like it." Mom turned the notebook toward me so I could see its contents. "But look..."

A few pages dense with cramped handwriting. Then nothing. The page torn out. Then another also torn out.

Shirley stared wide-eyed at the pages. "But why...?"

"Because Ken was about to tell the truth," I said. "And someone wanted to keep the truth buried."

"You think—?"

Mom snapped the notebook shut, cutting Shirley off. "Jack." She frowned. But a small smile quirked her lips. "We got him."

29

"Jack would never—" Trevor shook his head.

"We found Ken's notebook in his room," Mom said.

"No," Trevor repeated. "Not Jack..."

He was sitting on his bed in his room. I was leaning against the wall, my arms crossed. Mom stood next to Trevor, towering over him. He looked up, his big, puppy-ish eyes fixing on her. Pleading with her.

"We're all best friends," he said. "Why would Jack want to hurt Ken?"

"But are you really best friends?" I asked. "Ever since I saw Jack turn up at the church to pick up Ken, I've wondered. He wasn't there as a friend. He was there as an escort. A chaperone. To keep an eye on Ken."

"He was worried about Ken. See, Ken was—" Trevor grimaced and looked down at his hands. He was scratching the back of one hand. The skin was turning red. He added in a whisper, "—having a hard time."

"Did he even want to come to this year's reunion?" I asked.

Trevor stopped scratching his hand. Without looking up, he shook his head. "But it wouldn't be the same without Ken. Like it wouldn't be the same if any of us dropped out."

"But Ken did come," Mom said.

Trevor nodded. He looked up, a weak smile on his face. "I convinced him."

"You did?" Mom sounded skeptical. "How?"

"I went to visit him. Out of the blue. So he wouldn't make excuses and tell me to stay away. And I talked to him. I asked him to come. I just want us all to get along and hang out together. That's what I told him." Trevor cocked his head and stared off into the middle distance. "We were at his house in Palo Alto, sitting by the pool..."

I could almost picture it. The luminescent blue water. Ken in his sunglasses. Trevor all nervous energy, eager to please. Begging Ken to come. But what I couldn't imagine was Trevor barging in on Ken by himself.

"Was it your idea to visit Ken?" I asked.

Something flickered in Trevor's eyes. "Of course it was," he muttered. Looking down, he scratched his hand again. "I went to see Ken because he and I were buddies. Best buddies. And Jack went to talk to Judy."

"Because they were best buddies?"

Trevor shrugged. "We're all best buddies."

There was a knock at the door, and Mom went to it. I heard Deputy Douglas's voice. Then Mom said, "All right. We're done here, anyway." She turned back to us. "Trevor, we'll want to get your statement. Deputy Douglas and I will take Jack to the station to be booked."

Trevor jumped off his bed. "No," he said. "You can't do that."

"He attacked Shirley," I said. "And we found evidence in his suitcase. What did you expect?"

Trevor looked at me, his eyes wide, darting this way and that. "But what will happen to him?"

"A judge will decide that," Mom said and walked out of the room, leaving me behind with Trevor.

His lower lip trembled. He staggered back and collapsed onto the bed. With his elbows on his legs, he buried his face in his hands. "This was never supposed to happen..."

"Say what?"

He shook his head. "Nothing," he mumbled. "It's just..."

I went to him. I thought about sitting down next to him. But wouldn't he respond better to someone "in charge"? So I stood over him and put a hand on his shoulder.

"You need to tell me," I said.

Trevor gazed up at me, his big eyes welling with tears. "I can't..."

The door opened and someone bustled inside. He flinched back from me. I turned.

"Trevor," Judy said. "I heard what happened..."

She turned this way and that. Rummaged in her unruly hair. Straightened the scarf around her neck. Bags under her eyes suggested she hadn't slept well. She took a step toward me.

"We should—"

"No," Trevor said.

"If we don't—"

"You know we can't."

Judy shook her head. She turned to me. "I want to talk to you. And your mom. There's so much I want to say, and I don't even know where to begin."

Trevor's hand shot out. He grabbed Judy by the arm. She flinched. Her bangles jingling. Apparently, Trevor had a strong grip.

"No, Judy," he said.

The door opened again, and I turned. Priscilla came flying into the room, and when she saw the scene, she went straight to Judy. She stared daggers at Trevor.

"You let her go right now," she said.

Trevor dropped his hand as if it had been burned.

Priscilla put an arm around Judy and pulled her close.

"Come," she said, guiding Judy away. She glanced back over her shoulder at Trevor. Then she leaned close to Judy and whispered something. I caught some of it: "Trevor's losing it...not safe..." and "...keeping our distance..." and "...don't worry about Jack—he and I can vouch for each other..."

Then the door snapped shut. I turned to Trevor. His face had gone rigid. Tears trickled down his cheeks. He said, "I didn't do anything wrong..."

"What didn't you do wrong?"

He shook his head. Looked down. Unwilling to talk.

30

The Lakeview Inn was quiet. The night was quiet, too. Three hours had passed since Jack had been hauled down to the station. After all the excitement and the thumping of feet as people ran down corridors and stomped up and down stairs, it was a relief to sit in the lounge with Aunt Lil—just the two of us—and talk.

I'd sunk into an armchair, and Aunt Lil sat on the loveseat. Each of us with a cup of chamomile tea. With a hearty spoonful of honey from the Allington Woods.

"Where are they now?" Aunt Lil asked and sipped her tea.

"Trevor's probably where I left him in his room," I said. Then shrugged. "Priscilla must've whisked Judy off to either of their rooms—or maybe outside someplace."

"Priscilla seems like she spends a lot of time caring for everyone," Aunt Lil said.

I nodded. "They all seem to play a role in the group: Priscilla's the caring one; Trevor's the pleaser, wanting all his friends to get along; Judy is the jittery bird; and Jack is—"

I stopped myself. What was Jack? A snake? A shark? Or

maybe something less sinister, and just in the wrong place at the wrong time? His suspicious behavior, his attack on Shirley, and Ken's notebook pointed to him. But Priscilla's comments to Judy had reminded me of an important fact: Priscilla and Jack provided each other with alibis for the time of Ken's murder. Assuming they were both telling the truth...

I shook my head.

"What?" Aunt Lil asked.

"It's just that..." I sighed. "I don't like Jack. But something about all this smells fishy. I mean, if you killed Ken, would you keep his notebook lying around in your own room?"

"It does seem sloppy. And although Aries can be assertive, spontaneous, and adventurous, they are usually quick-witted."

I stared into my teacup. "So, why did the notebook turn up now?"

"Because the killer wanted it to?"

"Right. It was a form of insurance. If we started to get close to the truth, then the killer could plant it and—"

The door to the lounge cracked open. Priscilla stuck her head inside and looked around. She frowned.

"Have you seen Judy?"

"No," I said. "Not since the two of you left Trevor's room."

"Strange. I spent a few minutes with her in her room. Then she said she wanted to lie down and rest. But when I came back later, she didn't answer when I knocked."

"Her door's locked?"

"No, that's the thing. It's open. And she's not inside."

"Maybe she went for a walk," Aunt Lil suggested. "To clear her head."

"Yeah," Priscilla said, biting her lip. "That must be it."

She thanked us and withdrew, closing the door behind her.

I turned to Aunt Lil with a raised eyebrow. Aunt Lil shrugged and said, "Not every missing guest can mean trouble."

Our conversation turned to more mundane things: the preparation Aunt Lil had to do for more guests in the morning, the articles I had to write for *The Gazette*. But we were both dancing around our real thoughts. I certainly was. All I could think of was some detail I'd forgotten. Some very important detail. One that might crack this entire case wide open.

Just then, the door to the back porch cracked open.

Gordon Groff stood on the threshold, breathing heavily. His face glistening with sweat. His eyes wild.

"I swear," he panted. "I didn't—I didn't touch her."

I jumped to my feet, sloshing tea over my shirt. Aunt Lil carefully put down her cup and stood.

"Gordon," she said. "Take a deep breath and tell us what happened."

"Down there." He jabbed a thumb over his shoulder, gesturing out at the darkness. "She's down there. By the dock."

He swiveled around and trudged out onto the porch. Aunt Lil and I exchanged glances, then hurried after him.

Our footsteps—Aunt Lil's and mine—tapped on the floorboards of the porch. Groff's thumped. He headed down the stairs to the dock and we followed.

Halfway down the stairs, I stopped. My breath caught in my throat.

A shape floated in the dark water next to the dock. The end of her scarf undulating next to her.

Judy.

Groff reached the dock and turned around. He gazed up at us, his eyes pleading for understanding.

"She called me. Told me to come meet her here. Told me she could clear my name once and for all. I'm not making this up. I can show you the call log." He dug into his pocket, brought out a phone, and held it up. "I can prove it."

Why would he lie? But on the other hand, why would Judy call him? She had been repelled by Groff.

Yet there she was. Her dead body bobbing in the lake. Three hours ago, she'd been alive. Three hours ago, she'd desperately wanted to talk to me and Mom—she'd wanted to reveal the truth—and three hours ago, we'd missed the opportunity. We'd been too focused on Jack. Even on Trevor. Thinking we had all the time in the world to follow up.

I cursed under my breath.

Judy had reached out for help and I hadn't listened.

I'd let her down.

I'd let her die.

31

The quiet of the night was broken. The back porch of the inn and the dock below were bathed in a flood of light. The forensics team had set up lamps. They moved up and down the stairs. One of them sat in a boat that bobbed on the water as he scraped samples off the edge of the wooden dock. Judy's body had been pulled out and carted off long ago.

Mom and I stood by the lounge's windows. They were usually curtained, but Aunt Lil had opened up, so the three of us—me, Lil, and Mom—had a clear view.

"I should've gone straight to Judy," I whispered for the umpteenth time.

Behind us, several guests sat in the armchairs and on the loveseat, drawn to the lounge by the excitement. Some had checked out this evening, telling Aunt Lil that they were simply too afraid after so many bodies had been found in Allington. They would go stay at a motel on the highway. Who could blame them?

The only person to blame in all this was myself. I should've known. I should've done more to help Judy...

"You can't blame yourself," Mom said, a grim look on her face. "You're not the professional. I was the one who should've prioritized Judy."

"You had to focus on Jack. It's not like the police department has a big staff."

Mom shook her head. "Still..."

Behind us, two couples traveling together sat together. The women were huddled together, talking, occasionally casting glances our way. One of the husbands was hidden behind a copy of *The Gazette*, apparently preferring to read about Allington's latest birdwatching opportunities than to engage in the breaking news outside the windows. The second husband sat hunched over his phone, scrolling through audiobooks to listen to—also apparently bored by the drama outside—and occasionally accidentally tapping "play" so a voice would start talking: "...*different from his brothers and sisters. Their hair already betrayed the reddish hue inherited from their mother, the she-wolf; while he alone, in this particular, took after his father. He was the one little grey cub of the litter.*" He hit pause. Swiped again, apparently looking for another book. I'd already recognized snippets from books by Charles Dickens and James Fenimore Cooper.

His wife leaned forward and said, "Walt, will you put on those earbuds, please? You're being rude."

"Yeah, yeah, gimme a sec. Just finding a book I like."

His wife sighed and settled back into her conversation with her friend.

One of the Anglican priests came into the lounge and asked Aunt Lil about the evening bus. Aunt Lil explained that it left from across the street and, yes, it would stop at the small airport along the highway. The Anglicans, who had no car, were taking a small plane to their final destination.

After the conversation ended, Aunt Lil turned back to me and Mom. "The planetary alignments and the fate written in the palm of her hand decided the thing," she said with a finality that suggested the case was closed. "In any case, blaming yourselves won't bring back Judy. But her death must tell us something."

"You're right," Mom said, shedding her brief emotion. "It tells us the killer is getting desperate."

I thought about that. "I see it like this," I said. "The killer worried we were getting closer to the truth. So they hung Jack out to dry by planting Ken's notebook. Jack already looked suspicious because he attacked Shirley and because, well, he's Jack."

"Ain't that the truth," Aunt Lil said.

"But Trevor was beginning to crack," I said. "And Judy suddenly decided to spill the beans. Or else Trevor pretended to crack, while he was, in fact, keeping an eye on Judy. Who was becoming a risk. A risk worth eliminating."

"You think Trevor's the killer?" Mom asked.

I shook my head. "I don't know..."

"Priscilla and Trevor aren't leaving," Mom said. "We've clamped the wheels on their rental cars and made sure they're both in their rooms. If they killed Ken and Judy, we've got them where we want them."

If they killed them. I still wasn't sure. Jack was the one who'd made a show of following in Herman's footsteps, but who instead was covering the tracks, trying to convince everyone to look toward Mexico instead of Allington. That suggested Jack killed Herman. But Jack didn't set himself up. Plus, he had an alibi for the time of Ken's death. So either Jack killed Herman and someone else killed Ken, or—

The man sampling audiobooks played another preview. This time, a woman with an antiquated British accent read,

"In all England, I do not believe that I could have fixed on a situation so completely removed from the stir of society. A perfect misanthropist's Heaven—and Mr. Heathcliff and I are such a suitable pair to divide the desolation between us."

That must be a line from *Wuthering Heights* by Emily Brontë. Apparently, this story wasn't what the man was looking for either, because he sighed and continued his search.

But something about the sample he'd played made my mind burn.

"*...a suitable pair to divide the desolation between us,*" I muttered to myself. It was as if I'd heard that line before. Or heard the whole thing recently. From someone I knew. But how could that be? I didn't remember anyone around me reading *Wuthering Heights*. And suddenly an image flashed in my mind: a bottle of sleeping pills.

Mom was talking. So was Aunt Lil. But I didn't hear what they were saying. I was staring down at the blindingly bright lights on the crime scene by the dock.

That voice reverberated in my mind: "*...a suitable pair to divide the desolation between us.*" A voice I knew.

Then it came to me.

And I knew.

32

When Mom and I walked into her room, Priscilla was leaning over her suitcase on the bed, stuffing her clothes in. She grabbed a shirt from the bed and shoved it in. Then grabbed another. And another. Frantically filling the suitcase and then slamming it shut. The window stood open, the night breeze blowing in.

In her excitement, she hadn't heard us tiptoe inside.

She hefted the suitcase off the bed, straining against its weight. She took a step toward the window and glanced back. Maybe to make sure she hadn't forgotten anything.

She saw us.

She looked this way and that, and for a moment, her nervous movements reminded me of Judy. She hurried toward the window, frantically dragging the suitcase with her.

"You'll never get out that window," Mom said calmly. "And even if you do, we'll stop you before you get to that bus stop and board that bus."

Priscilla, one foot on the windowsill, froze.

"You're not going anywhere," Mom added.

Priscilla dropped her foot from the window. She stood still, her arms going limp. The suitcase bumped the floor as she dropped it.

Her eyes took on a dull look.

"Well," she said. "Go ahead and say it."

Mom stepped forward. A pair of handcuffs ready.

"Priscilla Nair, you're under arrest on suspicion of the murders of Judy Budgie and Ken Tora, and for conspiring to murder Herman Hertz."

After Mom had finished reading Priscilla her rights and cuffing her, Priscilla, looking and sounding bored, as if the whole incident was beneath her, said, "I'd like to call my lawyer."

Mom, taking Priscilla under the arm, escorted her out into the corridor.

Just then, Deputy Douglas emerged from another room, with Trevor in handcuffs. Trevor's face was twisted with emotion. Tears streaked his cheeks.

"Priscilla, I didn't tell them," he said breathlessly, "didn't tell them anything. They guessed. Somehow, they knew about Herman. And now they're saying you—"

"Shut up," Priscilla snapped.

Trevor's mouth closed. He stared at her wide-eyed.

"But Priscilla..." he said. "You told me the most important thing in the world was the Circle. Our friendship. That's why you told me to go get Ken. And why you told Jack to get Judy."

"Shut." Priscilla's face stiffened. "Up."

But Trevor seemed unable to stop. "Ken didn't want to go, but I did what you told me to—make it all about him and me, and our friendship. And in the end, he came. He came because of me."

"He came—" she spat. "—because of me. You all did. You fools would've given up years ago. You would've drunk too much and told someone. If it hadn't been for me and my insistence that we meet every year. I was the glue that held us together. Me. No one else."

"But Ken and Jack and Judy and me," Trevor said. "We're your friends."

"Friends," she scoffed. "We were never friends. We were allies. Conspirators. But what in the world could make us friends? We had nothing in common. Nothing." She laughed. A hard, bitter laugh. "Herman was the only one to see that. He knew it couldn't last. But the fool couldn't keep a secret. He had to tell someone. So he told Ken."

"And Ken told the rest of you," I said. "He warned you all about Herman, and so you tried to stop him."

Priscilla glanced at me and seemed to realize where she was and what she was doing. She grew tight-lipped and stared straight ahead, ignoring Trevor.

Trevor had gone still, too. He stared at her, wild-eyed.

"What happened?" I asked. "Did you all five plan to get rid of Herman?"

"It was an accident," Trevor said. "He and Jack got into a fight and he fell. He hit his head. And then we agreed it was better if we kept it quiet."

"So you buried Herman on Gull Island."

Trevor nodded, his eyes welling with tears. "We lit candles. Judy read a poem. It was beautiful."

Priscilla laughed again. "Beautiful," she scoffed.

Suddenly, Trevor leaped forward and Deputy Douglas had to fight to hold him back. Trevor strained on his cuffs. He fought. He snarled at Priscilla.

"You killed Ken and Judy. You killed my best friends. You promised we'd stick together. And then you killed them." He tried to rush at her, but Deputy Douglas dragged him back. Trevor yelled, "You're a murderer!"

Priscilla barked out a single laugh. "So are you. Didn't you throw as much dirt over Herman as I did?"

Trevor stopped struggling against Deputy Douglas's hold. His face crumpled. "I didn't...I never wanted him to..."

Priscilla looked at Mom. "Get me out of here. I can't take more of his blubbering."

Mom led him away. Deputy Douglas waited and then yanked Trevor's arm to get him walking. Trevor wept as he stared at the floor.

I watched them go.

33

"Now I understand why the sleeping pills were important," Aunt Lil whispered. "Priscilla drugged Jack so she could sneak out and kill Ken. That was why he was so groggy the morning we found Ken's body. But I still don't understand how the audiobook was the final clue."

We were sitting in a pew at church. Amy was on the dais, delivering a service about how showing up for others was showing up for yourself, and how showing up for yourself would ultimately help you show up for others. Aunt Lil sat to my right. Dad was on my left. Next to him sat Mom and on her other side sat Joy and then Ray and Roxie (a neighbor was watching Wimsey, their dog).

I leaned close to Lil. "Priscilla's voice. She was the voice artist for one of the books, and it made me realize that she had the skill to imitate others. Like the call to Groff from Judy. That's how she lured Groff to the docks in an attempt to frame him for killing Judy."

"Ah, now I see."

"Shhh…" Mom leaned forward and held a finger to her lips.

Aunt Lil grinned. "I love it when your mom polices us heathens in the pews."

I chuckled, shaking my head. "Oh, Aunt Lil."

But we both kept quiet and listened to Amy. She was quoting the Bible: "*Above all, love each other deeply, because love covers over a multitude of sins.*"

I thought of that. A lovely message. The members of the Circle hadn't loved each other. Apart for Trevor, maybe, the so-called friends feared each other and what each of them might do to reveal their past transgressions. In this case, fear had covered over a multitude of sins. Plagiarism. Cheating on exams. Stealing large amounts of money from churches. That fear had made them kill Herman. And having killed him, they had even more to lose if the truth came out.

I shook my head. The five of them—Ken, Jack, Judy, Priscilla, and Trevor—had been doomed from the beginning. There was no way to keep such secrets buried forever. Herman had realized it early on. Priscilla, too.

Amy talked about using our gifts to serve others, and it made me think of the Circle, and how each had used their skills to help the others. The study group had started with good intentions. But soon, it became corrupted. Its purpose was to cheat.

Now the Circle was finally broken. I leaned forward and spotted Manfred and Shirley in a pew further ahead. They would finally get some closure now. And not far from them sat a man in an old, floppy hat. A fisherman's hat. Gordon Groff?

But the man turned to talk to his companion, and I saw it wasn't Groff, after all.

No doubt Groff was holed up in his dark little cabin. All alone. And bitter.

Would he find closure now? I wasn't sure. I doubted it was in his nature, but maybe, just maybe, he'd find some small solace in knowing that the kids he'd suspected of wrongdoing had finally been caught. Maybe that would make him sleep better at night. Maybe it would even make him smile once in a while.

I glanced at Aunt Lil. She was listening to Amy with a smile on her face.

Amy was talking about the power of love—the love between friends and family—and how it could move mountains. And I thought of Aunt Lil and the rest of my family, and how our little circle was nothing but love.

Even if Mom shushed me in church on Sundays.

THANK YOU for reading this Parker Lee Mystery. Want more? Check out another mystery with Park and her family in:

Trouble Brewing

Want a **free short story**? Sign up for my newsletter to hear when the next book comes out and I'll share the story with you:

https://mpblackbooks.com/newsletter/

If you enjoyed this book, please take a moment to **leave a review online**. It makes it easier for other readers to find the book. Thanks so much!

Turn the page to read an excerpt from ***Trouble Brewing***...

34

EXCERPT FROM TROUBLE BREWING

"Oh, no," Ray groaned.

"What?" I asked.

"Break-in."

He pointed to the front door of the Breeze. Someone had crowbarred the lock, shattering the surrounding wood.

Ray stepped away from the door and cursed.

"They messed with the camera, too."

I looked up. A security camera perched on a brick ledge near the big sign that said, "Lake Breeze Brewery & Restaurant." But the burglar had covered the lens with what looked like a giant wad of gum.

"I'll call Mom," I said, digging my phone out of my pocket.

"Thanks," Ray said. "I'll call Roxie."

Roxie, Ray's wife, was his business partner. She managed the Breeze, handling finances and marketing, while my brother Ray took care of day-to-day operations at the bar and brewery. He was both co-owner and brewmaster.

I'd joined him this morning to get ideas for an article I'd

write for *The Allington Gazette* on the Breeze. It was Roxie's idea. Part of a marketing campaign they were running, which included posters throughout town. *The Gazette*, being a local paper, wasn't above giving local businesses a little extra love. Plus, it was my family. I wasn't above giving my family a little extra love.

But now this might turn into a front-page story about burglary instead.

Mom answered her cell phone. "Hey, Park."

In the background, I could hear voices, someone typing, and another phone ringing—the sounds of the Allington Police Department.

I told her about what happened and she promised to get down to the docks as quick as possible.

Ray said, "Let's go take a look at the damage."

"They can't have gotten away with much," I said, hoping to say something encouraging. "They'd need a boat to transport anything valuable. And that would be pretty conspicuous."

I gestured at the lake behind us. The Breeze occupied a brick building that used to be a warehouse for the lake trade back when Allington's biggest business was lumber. It was the town's favorite restaurant and bar. The place was often packed with tourists, every table under the awnings on the docks occupied—and locals gathered for dates and sports games and even the occasional wedding reception.

But this early on a Wednesday morning, the docks were abandoned. Out on the lake, a fisherman sat in his rowboat, patiently waiting for a catch. A bird dove into the water near Gull Island and then bobbed up again. The water shimmered. The sky was cloudless and blue. As if scrubbed clean after last night's rain.

"Guess we'll find out," Ray said, pulling open the door.

Inside, the bar and restaurant smelled of hardwood, beer, and barbecue. A good smell. As I followed Ray, I surveyed the space: the long wooden bar counter, the tables with the chairs stacked on top, and the booths. No sign of damage.

Ray went behind the bar and checked the liquor bottles.

"The burglar's been back here," he said. "Took a couple of bottles of bourbon."

"Expensive stuff?"

Ray shook his head. "I don't carry the cheapest brands, but this wasn't the premium stuff."

"What about the cash register?"

"It's open. Doesn't matter, though. It's empty." He shut the register with a bang. "We empty it every night and put the cash in our safe. The burglar must've been pretty disappointed."

"So the person just stole some bourbon and then bolted," I said. "That's not too bad."

"No, not too bad. We just have to fix the front door. But I'd better check the brewery."

I followed him to the back of the bar. A big sign on the door said, "DANGER: Staff Only." Ray pushed open the door. In the brewery, wooden floorboards gave way to white tile. A row of shiny metal tanks crowded the space. Pipes leading to each tank. More pipes criss-crossing the ceiling. On the side of each tank was a sign that said, "Danger: HOT."

At the far end, the ceiling opened, and the building expanded upward, leaving space for a row of massive fermentation tanks. They reminded me of silos.

Everything was tidy and clean.

"Looks fine," I said.

Ray rubbed the back of his neck, looking uncertain. "I

sure hope so. We've been brewing new batches and preparing for the weekend. We can hardly keep up with demand. Yesterday, we got everything ready for fermentation."

He wandered from tank to tank, checking gauges and looking behind the big metal kettles.

"This looks good," he said.

He moved down the brewery toward the back, and I followed him into the high-ceilinged area with the fermentation tanks. Ray stopped. A dead stop.

"Something's not right."

"What?"

I looked around. I saw nothing out of the ordinary. Everything was obsessively clean. Just those massive silo-like metal tanks.

Ray climbed a ladder to a narrow walkway along the tanks. I stayed below.

"No," he groaned, as he checked a set of gauges. "No, no, no..."

"What?"

He turned toward me. A look of despair on his face.

"The burglar must've messed with the thermostats." He turned back around, moving down the walkway to the next tank. He cursed. "This one, too. And this one, too."

Ray ran down the metal stairs and raced to a spigot at the bottom of one of the tanks. He grabbed a cup from a rack nearby and opened the spigot. Murky liquid spilled into the cup. He took a sip and grimaced.

"This can't be happening..."

He ran to the next vat and opened the spigot and tasted the beer there, too. And grimaced again.

"I don't get it," I said. "What happens if you tamper with the thermostats?"

Ray faced me. He leaned against the vat, as if to steady himself.

"It means trouble, Parker. The temperature's too high, which causes the yeast to produce more esters and phenols. The taste is way off. Plus, there's a risk of bacterial contamination."

"Which means...?"

"Which means we've got to start over. We've got to empty all the vats, throwing everything out." He ran a hand through his hair and let out a long breath. "This is a big blow to the business."

Want more? Grab *Trouble Brewing* at your favorite online bookstore.

MORE BY M.P. BLACK

A Wonderland Books Cozy Mystery Series

A Bookshop to Die For

A Theater to Die For

A Halloween to Die For

A Christmas to Die For

A Yarn Shop to Die For

A Hair Salon to Die For

An Italian-American Cozy Mystery Series

The Soggy Cannoli Murder

Sambuca, Secrets, and Murder

Tastes Like Murder

Meatballs, Mafia, and Murder

Parker Lee Mystery Series

The Art of Murder

The Deadly Circle

Trouble Brewing

A Killer View

Short stories

The Italian Cream Cake Murder (FREE)

ABOUT THE AUTHOR

M.P. Black writes fun cozies with an emphasis on food, books, and travel—and, of course, a good old murder mystery.

Besides writing and publishing his own books, he helps others fulfill their author dreams too through courses and coaching.

M.P. Black has lived in many places, including Brooklyn, Vienna, and San Jose de Costa Rica. Today, he and his family live in Copenhagen, Denmark, where coziness ("hygge") is a national pastime.

Join M.P. Black's free newsletter to download a free story and get updates on books and special deals:

https://mpblackbooks.com/newsletter/

www.ingramcontent.com/pod-product-compliance
Lightning Source LLC
LaVergne TN
LVHW051535170726
843492LV00006B/1775